Poptropica®

ASTRO-KNIGHTS
ISLAND

POPTROPICA

Published by the Penguin Group

Penguin Group (USA) Inc., 375 Hudson Street, New York, New York 10014, USA

Penguin Group (Canada), 90 Eglinton Avenue East, Suite 700,
Toronto, Ontario M4P 2Y3, Canada
(a division of Pearson Penguin Canada Inc.)

Penguin Books Ltd, 80 Strand, London WC2R 0RL, England

Penguin Ireland, 25 St Stephen's Green, Dublin 2, Ireland
(a division of Penguin Books Ltd)

Penguin Group (Australia), 707 Collins Street, Melbourne, Victoria 3008, Australia
(a division of Pearson Australia Group Pty Ltd)

Penguin Books India Pvt Ltd, 11 Community Centre,
Panchsheel Park, New Delhi—110 017, India

Penguin Group (NZ), 67 Apollo Drive, Rosedale, Auckland 0632, New Zealand
(a division of Pearson New Zealand Ltd)

Penguin Books, Rosebank Office Park,
181 Jan Smuts Avenue, Parktown North 2193, South Africa

Penguin China, B7 Jaiming Center, 27 East Third Ring Road North,
Chaoyang District, Beijing 100020, China

Penguin Books Ltd, Registered Offices: 80 Strand, London WC2R 0RL, England

© 2007–2012 Pearson Education, Inc. All rights reserved.
Published by Poptropica, an imprint of Penguin Young Readers Group,
345 Hudson Street, New York, New York 10014. Printed in the U.S.A.

ISBN 978-0-448-46199-1   10 9 8 7 6 5 4 3 2 1

ALWAYS LEARNING   PEARSON

Poptropica®

ASTRO-KNIGHTS
ISLAND

adapted by Tracey West
cover illustrated by Angel Rodriguez
illustrated by Robert Roper

Poptropica
An Imprint of Penguin Group (USA) Inc.

Chapter One

Strange Disks in the Sky

Cock-a-doodle-doo!

Simon Cobb groaned at the sound of the rooster's loud morning crow.

If he had a pillow, he would have pulled it over his head, rolled over, and gone back to sleep. But the young stable boy slept on a thin mattress stuffed with straw, without a pillow or even a blanket. Besides, he didn't want to be late for work. That always put Edmund, the stable master, in a bad mood—and working in the stable was bad enough without Edmund stomping around.

He yawned and stood up, brushing a strand of brown hair from his eyes. The rooster strutted through the hut's open door and stared at Simon with accusing yellow eyes.

"Give me a break," Simon told the rooster. "The sun's not even up all the way."

A red-haired girl poked her head inside the hut. "Aren't you up yet, Simon?" asked Alice.

"It's not even daytime yet," Simon protested. "Anyway, why aren't you in the Castle?" Simon didn't know much about Alice's job in the Castle as a scullery maid, but he knew she had to be up even earlier than he did to help make breakfast for everyone in the royal court.

"I snuck out," she said, stepping inside. Her green eyes were shining. "I thought you'd want to know—the knights are riding out today!"

The news jolted Simon awake. Nothing much exciting happened out in the stables, but he always loved it when the knights came. Sir Pelleas, Sir Cador, and Sir Gawain were the superstars of Arturus. They were tall and strong, and they lived exciting lives, protecting the kingdom from danger.

Simon had been eagerly awaiting their next visit to the stables. He hoped to impress them so that one of them might make him a squire. Then he'd be able to leave the muck and horse manure behind and travel with the knights, helping them—and maybe even riding his own horse.

"They're riding out? Where?" Simon asked. He ran past Alice to the water bucket outside and splashed cold water on his face. The hut didn't have a mirror, so he gazed at his reflection in the water. He scrubbed a patch of dirt off his cheek and used some more water to smooth down a lock of hair sticking up on top of his head.

Alice shook her head. "Are you actually trying to impress them?"

"Just watch. I'm going to be a squire someday," he said confidently. "I'm not going to spend my whole life mucking out stables. I'm going to have a horse of my own."

"Well, you'd better let me ride it, then," Alice said. "I never get to do anything fun."

She thrust a hunk of bread and a hard-boiled egg into his hands.

"From the kitchens," she said. "Those royals have more food than they need."

"Thanks," Simon said.

His friend grinned. "No problem. Good luck impressing the knights! I'd better get back before they figure out I'm gone."

Alice ran off, and Simon shoved the breakfast in his mouth as he headed in the other direction. He sprinted across the field, the moist grass squishing under his bare feet. He lived close to the stables, which was a good thing when he was late and a bad thing when a breeze sprung up, sending the smell of manure

his way. Simon swore he'd never get used to the smell as long as he lived.

When he arrived at the stables, he saw Edmund, the stable master, carrying a heavy bucket of water.

"I'll take that," Simon said quickly, but Edmund pushed him away.

"Go find Tobias," Edmund said gruffly. "He needs some help mucking out the stalls in the back."

Simon sighed and made his way to the back stalls. Three horses were tied to posts outside, and from inside the stalls Simon heard a familiar song.

"Muck, muck, muck, oh yes, it's time to muck."

Simon grabbed a shovel and headed toward the song. Tobias, the other stable boy, greeted him with a cheerful smile.

"Good morning, Simon," he said. "Isn't it a beautiful day?"

It wasn't right to call Tobias a stable boy, exactly.

At twenty-seven years old, he was practically an old man. He'd been working in the stables since he was five, and he loved his job more than anything.

"Um, yeah, it's nice out, I guess," Simon mumbled. "So, Tobias, I heard the knights are coming today."

Tobias nodded. "That's right. Gotta get the stables nice and clean!"

"Do you know where they're going?" Simon asked.

Tobias shrugged. "Agnes down at the mill said that the King was sending them to look for Mordred again. But you know how it is. You never can believe everything you hear at that mill. It's a regular rumor mill, it is."

Simon nodded. The lazy gossips at the mill spread a lot of crazy stories around Arturus, but the stories about Mordred the inventor were the craziest. Simon never paid too much attention to them. Some people in the village practically worshipped

the guy, but Simon thought Mordred's fans were fools. In his eyes, Sir Pelleas, Sir Cador, and Sir Gawain were the only heroes that Arturus needed.

"Well, if the knights really are going after Mordred, I'm sure they'll get him," Simon assured Tobias.

A dark look crossed Tobias's face. "If you ask me, I hope he stays lost," he replied. Then his smile returned. "Best get back to mucking! Muck, muck, muck! Muck, muck, muck!"

Simon lifted his shovel and began to fill a wheelbarrow with mounds of stinky horse manure. The more he shoveled, the dirtier he got. He'd never make a good impression on the knights now.

"We're full up!" Tobias called out, dumping one last shovelful into the wheelbarrow.

"I'll take it," Simon offered. He grabbed the wood handles and pushed away from the stables.

All the manure was composted in the muddy field behind the windmill. In the spring, the farmers would use it to cover the fields. Until then, it was just one big, stinking mess.

At least it's a nice day, Simon thought as he pushed the wheelbarrow. There was nothing worse than mucking out a stable in the rain. He looked up. The yellow sun shone against a blue sky dotted with puffy white clouds and shiny silver disks.

"Shiny silver disks?" Simon stopped in his tracks and shaded his eyes against the sun. What were those things? Birds?

The disks got closer and closer to Arturus, and Simon saw that they didn't look natural. They looked man-made.

He stared, frozen, as the flying disks hovered in the Arturus sky. Then round, flaming balls shot out from the disks, and Simon realized they were aimed right at the kingdom.

Something deep inside him kicked in, and he ran behind the nearest manure pile and ducked, covering his head with his hands.

Boom! Boom! Boom!

All around him, the world began to explode.

Chapter Two

Attacked!

After the first blast of fear subsided, Simon's natural curiosity took over. He cautiously peeked around the manure pile and gazed at the sky.

The flying disks had swooped down closer, almost grazing the tall turrets of the Castle. Beams of fiery red light shot from the disks, and whatever the light touched exploded into bits.

Is it fire? Simon wondered. Maybe the disks were some kind of strange dragon. But the red light was much more powerful and controlled than fire. Once again, he got the feeling that they were dealing with something unnatural.

"To the horses!"

A rousing cry came from the direction of the stables. Simon recognized Sir Cador's voice immediately, and he realized that the knights were mounting up to fight the invaders. He had to help them! He darted out from behind the manure pile and raced for the stables.

Boom! One of the fiery blasts hit the ground just a few feet to Simon's right, sending dirt and muck flying. His heart beat faster than it ever had before. This was danger like he'd never seen. But he couldn't fail the knights.

He pounded the dirt, running as fast as he could. *Boom!* Another blast rocked the earth behind him, and Simon dove through the stable door, landing in a soft pile of hay.

The commotion inside the stable was almost louder than the chaos outside; the horses were bucking and rearing, terrified. Edmund stomped around them, screaming for them to calm down, which only made things worse.

"Quiet, man!" Sir Pelleas barked angrily. "We must ride out immediately to save the kingdom!"

Simon quickly raced to the sturdy chestnut warhorse Edmund was tormenting and grabbed its bridle.

"It's okay, Roland," he said, gently stroking the horse's nose. "Sir Pelleas needs you. The kingdom is in danger."

The horse immediately calmed down, and Tobias quickly moved to help Sir Pelleas mount the horse. The knight lifted his visor and nodded at Simon.

"Good work, boy," he said approvingly. "Now see to the others."

"Yes, sir!" Simon replied, bursting with pride. Sir Pelleas had actually spoken to him! Next he calmed Sir Gawain's white steed and Sir Cador's black one.

The three knights looked magnificent mounted on their horses, Simon thought: Sir Pelleas in his shining orange armor, Sir Gawain in his ice-blue armor, and Sir Cador in his green armor.

Then a loud cry came from outside the stables. "The invaders are attacking the Castle!"

"We must save our king!" Sir Pelleas exclaimed. "Let us ride!"

The knights spurred on their horses, and they galloped out of the stables toward the Castle. Simon started to run after them.

"Where are you going, boy?" Edmund barked. "It's not safe out there!"

"I've got to find Alice!" Simon called back as he raced off to look for his friend.

Boom! Boom! Boom! The flying disks—about a dozen of them, Simon guessed—were focusing their

attack on the Castle now. He watched in horror as one of the stone turrets crumbled to pieces, sending chunks of rock tumbling to the ground below.

"Alice!" he yelled, picking up his pace.

"Over here!"

To his relief, he saw Alice waving to him, safe behind a haystack. He quickly ran to her.

"You okay?" he asked.

She nodded. "We thought we'd be safe down in the kitchen. But then one of those blasts came right through the ceiling! Missed me by inches. So I got out of there, fast."

"So who's attacking us?" Simon asked. "And what do they want with the Castle?"

Alice shrugged. "I don't know. But they definitely don't seem to like Arturus very much."

Simon watched, holding his breath, as the knights charged at the invaders with their lances. Although the flying disks were hovering lower than before, the knights still couldn't reach them. The invaders shot fiery blasts at the knights, but the skilled horsemen rode circles around the attacks.

"We can't reach them!" Sir Gawain cried out.

Sir Cador eyed the large crossbow stationed on a landing above the Castle door.

"Oh yes, we can!" he called back.

Sir Cador galloped to the door, dodging blasts, and then jumped off his horse, grabbing the ledge above the door. He swung up to the platform and loaded the crossbow with a long, heavy arrow. He pulled it back, aiming for a disk hovering above one of the Castle towers.

Ziiiing! The arrow zoomed through the air, penetrating its target with massive force. The disk careened wildly in the air before crashing into one of the towers, sending a billowing plume of smoke into the blue sky.

"Huzzah!" Sir Cador cried, and then he loaded the crossbow again.

"Go, Cador!" cheered Simon and Alice from behind the haystack.

Sir Pelleas rode up beside Sir Gawain. "We must combine the power of our arrows," he said. Sir Gawain nodded with understanding. They loaded their bows and then hit another of the disks with a barrage of arrow fire. The smaller arrows didn't have the same power as the arrow in the crossbow and couldn't penetrate the flying craft's metal shell.

But the rain of arrows seemed to confuse the disk. It lurched to avoid the arrows and knocked into a tree, sending sparks flying. Damaged, the craft wobbled away from the Castle and flew toward the windmill.

Simon and Alice high-fived each other.

"Another one down!" Simon exclaimed.

Then Alice nudged him. "Look! They're flying away!"

It was true. The remaining disks zoomed up and away from the Castle into the blue sky, leaving plumes of black smoke streaming from the Castle. Simon and Alice cautiously stepped out from behind the haystack, along with other curious villagers.

"The knights have defeated the invaders!" some yelled, and a cheer went up from the crowd. Simon joined in with a loud whistle. Nobody could beat the knights!

But the onlookers suddenly quieted down as the Queen stepped out of the Castle door. Her red robe was singed and dirty, and tendrils of her usually neat blond hair stuck out from behind her crown.

"The Princess has been kidnapped!" she cried.

Chapter Three

The Mystical Weapons

Word of the missing Princess quickly spread throughout Arturus. Soon the Castle grounds were crowded with the puzzled and concerned citizens of the kingdom. Dairymaids stopped milking cows, peasants stopped weeding the fields, and bakers left their ovens empty as they gathered to hear the news.

After the disks flew off, Simon had gone back to the stables to tend to the horses, panting and sweaty after their charge. When they were watered, fed, and groomed, Simon hurried back to the grounds to find out what was happening.

The murmuring voices of the villagers rumbled like thunder across the grounds as everyone talked at once.

"The invaders blew my roof clear off!"

"They came from beyond the stars!"

"I'll bet Mordred had something to do with this!"

Simon scanned the crowd, quickly spotting Alice's mop of red hair. He squeezed past a group of pitchfork-wielding peasants and tapped her on the shoulder.

"Hey," he said.

"Hey," she replied. "You should see what's going on inside. The Castle guards are telling crazy stories. One guy says he saw little green men inside those disk things."

"Leprechauns?" Simon asked. "I didn't know they could fly."

Alice shrugged. "Who knows? Another guard says the disks were empty, like they had minds of their own."

"Metal dragons!" Simon guessed. "I knew it!"

"But the lady-in-waiting has the craziest story of all," Alice went on. "She's the one who saw the Princess being kidnapped. She says the man who took her was half human, but the other half of him was made of metal!"

"Really?" Simon asked, his eyes wide. "Do you think she's telling the truth?"

"Maybe," Alice said. "That makes as much sense as anything else. I mean, it's not every day that invaders come down from the sky."

Simon nodded. "True. This is all so weird."

"I feel bad for the Princess, but honestly, it's kind of fun," Alice admitted with a guilty smile. "I mean, nobody got hurt, really. And it's been so boring around here since the power went out."

There hadn't been any power in Arturus since the day Mordred left.

"I didn't really notice," Simon said with a shrug. "I never had power in my hut, anyway. And you don't need electricity to clean out a stable."

"Well, I definitely miss it," Alice countered. "It's so much harder to cook and clean without Mordred's inventions to help us. That's why I have to get up so early."

The sound of a trumpet interrupted them, and the crowd grew silent as the King stepped out onto the balcony of the Castle.

Like the Queen, the King's red, fur-trimmed robes were singed and dirty, and Simon thought he could see some new gray hairs growing in his once-brown beard.

The three knights stepped out onto the balcony and stood respectfully behind the King.

"Citizens of Arturus!" the King began in a booming voice. "Today has been a grievous day. Our kingdom has been attacked by invaders from the sky. And while our knights bravely fended them off, the invaders kidnapped my beloved daughter, Princess Elyana."

A gasp went up from the crowd. Most of them had heard the story, but hearing the King say it made it real.

"But in darkness, there is hope," the King went on. "These brave knights, Sir Pelleas, Sir Gawain, and Sir Cador, have sworn to bring the Princess back to Arturus. They will travel to the stars in one of the flying crafts they helped bring down during the battle."

A cheer went up from the crowd, and Simon and Alice joined in.

"Go, knights! Go, knights! Go, knights!"

The King motioned for everyone to quiet down.

"Our knights will not go into this dangerous

territory unarmed," he said. "For today, I will bestow on them the Three Mystical Weapons of Arturus!"

The villagers began to chatter with excitement.

"I've heard stories about them, but I didn't think they were real," Simon said.

"Well, I guess we're about to find out," Alice replied.

Three Castle servants walked onto the balcony, each one carrying an object on a red silk pillow. The King removed the first object, a golden crystal hanging from a cord. He slipped it over Sir Gawain's head.

"For you, Sir Gawain, this Force Shield," said the King. "It will protect you from harm."

Sir Gawain bowed. Then the King took the second item, a blue arrow, and handed it to Sir Pelleas.

"For you, Sir Pelleas, this Ice Arrow," the King said. "This weapon will counter fiery attacks."

Sir Pelleas bowed, and the King picked up the third object, the largest of the three weapons—a long, green lance with a point at the end.

"Sir Cador, the Laser Lance is yours," the King said, handing it to him. "It is capable of shooting blasts as powerful as those fired by the invaders."

Sir Cador bowed and proudly held the lance in the

air. He stepped forward.

"For Arturus!" he cried, and the crowd cheered and clapped.

"Those weapons are amazing," Alice said. "I would love to try using that lance, wouldn't you?"

Simon nodded. "Or that Ice Arrow. I've got pretty good aim, you know."

The Castle musicians began to play a rousing song, and everyone made their way to the field next to the Castle, where some more servants were polishing one of the crashed flying disks, which rested on a crudely built wooden platform. Soon the knights made their way through the crowd followed by the King and Queen.

The servants raised the clear dome on top of the craft, and the three knights stepped inside. Before he entered, Sir Pelleas bent down and kissed the Queen's hand.

"We will not fail you, my lady," he promised.

"Godspeed, Pelleas," she said. "Godspeed to all of you."

The dome closed on the knights, and Simon saw Sir Gawain pressing something inside the craft.

"I wonder how they know how it works," he mused out loud.

"Maybe it comes with instructions," Alice suggested. "Or maybe they really did capture one of those little green pilots, and *he* told them."

Simon shook his head. "I'll say it again. This is all really weird!"

Suddenly a loud sound came from the craft, like the whir of a motor, and the disk began to rise from the platform. The villagers cheered and waved good-bye, and the flying disk shot up into the sky, quickly becoming a glinting silver dot against the blue. Then it disappeared.

"I wonder if we'll ever see them again," Alice mused.

"Of course we will!" Simon said confidently. "The Knights of Arturus will never be defeated!"

Chapter Four

The Mordred Museum

"The Knights of Arturus have been defeated," Alice said. "At least, that's what the gossips in the mill are saying."

"They don't know what they're talking about," Simon insisted. "The knights will come through, I just know it."

But even as he said the words, Simon felt a twinge of doubt. The knights had been gone for days now. Every day, he stared up at the sky, waiting for them to return. And every night, he fell asleep disappointed.

The two friends were sitting on a fence by the stables, underneath that same blue sky. As peasants, they very rarely got a day off, and when they did, they tried to spend it together.

"So what do you want to do today?" Simon asked.

"Well . . ." Alice said slowly. "I was thinking we could go to the Museum of Mordred."

Simon made a face. "You know I don't care about that guy. All those stories are a bunch of nonsense."

"But they're an interesting bunch of nonsense," Alice countered. "And, anyway, I think you need to take your mind off those knights. I can tell how worried you are."

Simon hopped down from the fence. "I am *not* worried," he lied. "But since it's your turn to pick what we do, I'll go."

Alice jumped down, landing next to him. "Cool! You won't regret it, Simon."

They walked toward the Castle, heading away from the stench of the stables and the muddy field. As they made their way along the grassy path they jumped over jagged craters in the dirt, still fresh from the attack. On the main road in the village, the shingled walls of the Crop Circle Inn were singed and the Planetarium next door had a broken window.

When they got to the museum, a small stone house with a wood roof, Simon suddenly realized something.

"Hey, we can't go here," he said. "Doesn't it cost a coin to get in?"

"No problem," Alice said. "There are always coins in the fountain."

She ran to the elaborate granite fountain that Mordred's fans had constructed next to the museum. The fountain's base was round, with another round pool on a platform rising up from the center. And rising from the second pool was a spacecraft carved from stone, with a twisted trail of smoke connecting the craft to the fountain. Water flowed into the pool from three small tubes at the end of the craft.

Alice jumped into the fountain and began to splash around, looking for coins.

"So what is this thing supposed to be?" Simon asked.

"Mordred's worshippers call it a rocket," she said. "They say it's what he used to escape to the stars."

Simon shook his head. "Ridiculous."

"I thought so, too," Alice said. "Until we got attacked from the sky. Hey, two coins!"

She flipped a coin down to Simon and jumped out of the fountain. Simon sighed.

"What a waste of a perfectly good coin."

"It'll be fun," Alice said, dragging him by the arm. "Come on!"

Inside the museum, the curator greeted them with a sneer of disdain. A pale man with a neatly trimmed red beard, he was dressed in fine purple trousers and a matching velvet hat. He clearly had no time for peasants.

"Sorry," he said. "You need one coin to enter."

"Not a problem," Alice said with a grin, handing him her coin. Simon reluctantly turned over his as well.

"So do we get to see Mordred's secret stuff?" Alice asked eagerly.

The curator rolled his eyes. "This is not Mordred's laboratory. This is his home."

"Before the king imprisoned him, you mean," Simon mumbled.

The curator ignored him. "What you see is what you get. Enjoy your visit."

Alice began to walk around the first floor, which held a bunch of books, a lot of cobwebs, and Mordred's old computer—which would have been interesting if it could work. Nothing worked anymore since the power went out.

"Wow, this is fascinating," Simon said sarcastically. "Definitely worth the price of admission."

He quickly felt bad for saying it when he saw Alice's disappointed expression.

"Hey, maybe there's something cool upstairs," he said, pointing to a loft overhead. Alice grinned.

"Let's climb up!"

But in the loft they found only more cobwebs, more books, Mordred's old bed, and a lot of dust.

"Okay! You were right! This is boring," Alice admitted. "Let's get out of here and go hang out by the creek or something."

They climbed down from the loft. Simon felt bad for his friend. As they headed to the door, he walked over to a table full of books.

"Hey, these could be interesting," he said. "Maybe we can borrow one and read it by the creek."

The curator quickly stepped up to him. "No, no, I'm very sorry. The books cannot leave the museum."

Simon was feeling frustrated. He spotted a slip of paper sticking out of one of the books. It was an old library slip with Mordred's signature on it.

"Well, I think we deserve at least a souvenir after what we paid," he argued. "Can we take this old library slip?"

The curator sighed. "Very well. If you promise to be on your way."

"Oh, we promise," Simon said. "Come on, Alice, let's go."

When they got outside, Simon handed the slip to Alice.

"See? It's got Mordred's autograph on it," he said.

"Excellent!" Alice said with a grateful smile. "Sorry if I ruined your day. Let's go to the creek."

"Sure," Simon said, stepping forward. Then he stopped. "Hey, what's that?"

Two mysterious figures in hooded purple robes were approaching the fountain. The hoods were pulled low, covering their faces.

"Bandits?" Alice whispered. "We should be careful."

The two friends flattened themselves against the front wall of the museum, hoping the robed figures would pass by without seeing them. But after a few seconds, there was no sign of the figures. Curious, Simon peered around the wall.

The figures were gone.

"That's weird," Simon said. "Where did they go?"

"It's almost like they disappeared inside the fountain," Alice remarked. She walked up and started to examine it. "But I don't see a door or anything."

"No, there's just this plaque," Simon said. Carved into a plaque mounted on the second pool were the words: "In Memory of Mordred, Who Brought

Technology to Our Land, but Went Astray."

"If he went astray, then why build him a statue?" Simon wondered.

"Some people don't agree with the King," Alice said. "He thought Mordred's experiments were evil. But Mordred's fans thought the King was being close-minded. They thought Mordred was a genius."

"Do you think those people in the purple robes were Mordred worshippers?" Simon wondered.

"Maybe," Alice said. "It's definitely weird."

Simon nodded in agreement. "Definitely!"

Chapter Five

Simon Steps Up

Simon's day off seemed to fly by. Before he knew it, he was back in the stables, shoveling manure again. Tobias, as usual, was singing his mucking song.

"I need someone to take a message to the Castle for me," Edmund said late that afternoon, stomping up to the stables. He looked Tobias and Simon up and down, and must have decided that Simon looked slightly cleaner. "Here you go, Simon. Don't be long."

Simon gratefully put down his pitchfork and took the scroll of paper with a nod. It didn't take very long to get a message to the Castle—he'd usually just hand it to a footman and leave—but he was hoping to make the errand last as long as he could.

He slowly meandered along the path, whistling a tune until he reached the Castle steps. Then he smoothed down his hair, plucking out a few strands of hay, and climbed the steps.

Only then did he realize how strange things were—normally, the Castle guards would have stopped him before letting him enter, and the footman would have greeted him. But it was like the Castle had been frozen in time since the day the Princess was kidnapped. A cold breeze blew through the holes the invaders had blasted in the walls. The few servants he could see walked around like zombies, sad and distracted. He tried to approach one of them, but the man walked away, ignoring him.

What now? Simon wondered. If he didn't deliver the message, Edmund would surely yell at him and probably give him extra duties. He couldn't fail. So he made his way up to the second floor, waiting for a guard to stop him.

But he entered the throne room without anyone giving him a second glance. The once-grand room was in shambles. Sunlight streamed through a huge hole in the wall, and the King and Queen sat on their thrones, with the Princess's empty throne between them. The Queen looked like she had been crying for days.

"Ex-excuse me," Simon said nervously. "But I have a message from Edmund the stable master for you."

"Message?" the King asked absently. "Oh, yes. Thank you."

Simon cautiously approached the throne and

handed the scroll to the King. The poor King and
Queen looked so heartbroken that something
moved Simon to speak.

"Excuse me, Your Highnesses, but is
everything all right?" he asked.

"Of course it's not all right!" the Queen wailed.
"My daughter is gone! Gone to the fabric beyond the
sky!" Then she began to sob.

"But surely the knights will rescue her," Simon said.

The King shook his head. "It has been many days since the knights left. I fear they are lost. We shall never see Elyana again. If only some brave soul would step up to follow them and find our daughter!"

"Surely one of the Castle guards will do it," Simon suggested.

"There is no one brave enough," the King replied dismally. "That is why my servants and guards hide in the shadows. They are afraid I will send them into the sky."

Something welled up inside Simon at that moment, and the words were out of his mouth before he realized he was saying them. "I will do it," he offered. "I will rescue the Princess!"

Chapter Six

A Mystery . . . and a Mouse

The King raised an eyebrow. "You? A stable boy?"

"I may be a stable boy now, but I don't plan to be one forever," Simon said, once again surprised by his own words. It was like a can of courage and confidence had been opened up inside him, and now it was all spilling out. "And none of your guards are brave enough to go, but I will. I'm not afraid."

The King stood up, walked over to Simon, and carefully studied his face.

"No, I don't believe you are afraid," he said. "Very well, then. Find my daughter, and I shall make you a knight!"

"A knight?" Simon couldn't believe it. All his life he'd dreamed of being a squire . . . but a knight? He tried to imagine himself riding tall on one of the stable's finest horses, clad in shining armor.

Of course, he'd have to find the Princess first.

Simon bowed. "I will not fail you," he said, in the most important voice he could muster.

The queen approached him. "You will need these," she said, slipping three sheets of paper into his hand.

Simon studied them. Each one had strange markings. X-73, Y-83. X-15, Y-15. X-83, Y-20.

The queen noticed his puzzled expression. "They are coordinates. The knights left them with us."

"Coordinates . . . you mean like points on a map?" Simon asked.

She nodded. "Before they left in the flying disk, the knights charted a course to three planets in the heavens. The Princess must be on one of them."

This is too good to be true, Simon thought. *I just have to follow the coordinates, and I'll find the knights—and maybe even the Princess.*

"Great!" Simon said. "So I just need to hop in a flying disk, and I'll be on my way."

"Did you think it would be that easy?" the King asked. "You must find a way to get to space on your own. The knights took the only working flying disk the invaders left behind."

Simon's heart sank. How could he rescue the Princess from outer space if he couldn't get there?

The Queen frowned and turned to her husband. "Richard, perhaps the boy may find some solution in Mordred's old laboratory."

The King's face darkened. "How dare you mention that name in this Castle? That evil man's darkness cannot help us now."

"But Elyana's life is at stake," the Queen pleaded. "Surely we must—"

"Arguing does not become you, my love," the King said firmly. "I will hear no more of this. Let us see what the boy can do."

Simon instinctively bowed again. "Yes, Your Highness," he said. "Is there anything else you can tell me about the kidnapping? Do you know who took the Princess, or why?"

The Queen sadly shook her head. "Elyana had been acting very strangely of late, spending long hours in her room. But I do not know why."

"Thank you," Simon said. "So I guess I'll be on my way then."

The Queen smiled at him. "Godspeed, young man."

Simon turned to leave, then quickly turned back.

"I almost forgot something," he said. "My friend Alice works as a scullery maid in the Castle. Can she come with me?"

"If you wish," the King said.

Simon turned again but changed his mind once more.

"And when we bring back the Princess, can she become a knight, too?" Simon asked.

The King sighed. "You may be a mere stable boy, but you negotiate like a lawyer. Yes, if you and your friend succeed, you shall both be knighted."

"Thanks!" Simon said. "You can count on us!"

Simon bounded out of the throne room and back down the stone stairs, his mind spinning. What was he thinking? He had no idea how to get into space, and when he did, how was he supposed to find the Princess? The knights had tried and failed. What made him think he could succeed?

"Alice is never going to believe this," he muttered. Or Edmund, for that matter.

Thinking of Edmund made Simon more afraid than the thought of going into space. Edmund was going to be pretty angry that Simon was leaving work to look for the Princess. If he succeeded, it wouldn't matter. But if he failed, he'd have to go crawling back, begging for his job.

I won't fail, Simon told himself. *I can't fail.*

As he made his way to the basement kitchen, he saw a young woman in a blue gown walking into one of the first-floor rooms. She wore a crisp white scarf draped over her head, held in place by a blue band.

It was Rose, the Princess's lady-in-waiting. He had seen her a few times with Princess Elyana, when she had come to the stables to ride. He suddenly remembered what Alice had said—that a half robot, half man had kidnapped the Princess. Maybe she knew something that could help him.

Simon gently knocked on the door.

"Pray, come in."

Inside, Rose was seated at her dressing table, staring into the mirror with a forlorn look on her face.

"Pardon me, miss," Simon said. "But the King has sent me to find Princess Elyana, and I thought maybe you could help me."

"You?" Rose asked sharply, snapping out of her melancholy.

"Yes, me," Simon said. "I heard that you saw who kidnapped the Princess."

Rose shuddered. "I dare not speak of it further. That day feels like a terrible nightmare now."

He could see that Rose didn't want to talk. But he knew that she and the Princess were good friends. At the stables, they were always talking and whispering secrets to each other.

"But don't you want to help find the Princess?" Simon asked. "You must know something."

Rose turned to Simon, her eyes wide. "Promise you will tell no one?" she asked.

"Promise," Simon said, crossing his fingers behind his back. He would have to tell Alice, of course, but he didn't feel like explaining that now, not when Rose was ready to talk.

"I . . . I fear I may have played a part in the Princess's kidnapping!" she said and then broke into a sob.

"What do you mean?" Simon asked.

Rose dried her eyes with a handkerchief. "Elyana was using me to deliver messages to a secret society." She opened her drawer, took out a piece of paper, and handed it to Simon. "This is the last one, but I never got to deliver it."

Simon studied the message.

We must change our password. I fear my parents suspect what we are doing.

Things were getting interesting. "Secret society? Where? Did you see them?" Simon asked.

Rose shook her head. "No. I left them at the fountain in the town square."

The same fountain where Alice and I saw those purple-robed people, Simon thought.

"Thank you," he said. Then he got an idea. "Hey,

do you think I could look in the Princess's room? Maybe she left some clues there."

"It is locked," Rose informed him. "The King and Queen have forbidden anyone to enter. In their grief, they want to keep it as she left it. Even I cannot get in."

"Okay," Simon said. "Then I'll just be—hey!"

He jumped as something skittered across his foot. Looking down, he saw a silver mouse darting under Rose's bed. Simon knelt down to get a better look.

"Is that a mechanical mouse?" he asked.

"One of Mordred's creations," Rose explained. "Horrid little thing. I can't seem to get rid of it."

"That's too bad," Simon said. "Guess I'd better be going."

"Good luck!" Rose called after him. "I hope you find her!"

Simon went down another flight of stairs and entered the busy Castle kitchen. He spotted Alice on her hands and knees, scrubbing the floor with a rag. Mary, the plump Castle cook (Alice always said she had the shape of a tomato), was standing over her.

"You missed a spot! Honestly, Alice, I don't know

what to do with you sometimes," she said with a click
of her tongue.

"You don't have to do anything with her," Simon
said, stepping up. "She's coming with me. By the order
of the King."

Alice looked up at him, a mix of curiosity and
admiration on her face.

Mary shooed him away with her hand. "Get
out of here, you smelly stable boy. And stop talking
nonsense."

"It's not nonsense," Simon said. "The King said
that Alice could come with me to find the Princess."

"He did?" Alice asked.

Simon nodded. "I am serious. Come on, let's get out of here."

Alice tossed the rag on the floor and jumped up.

"You don't have to ask me twice!"

Chapter Seven

The Disciples of Mordred

Simon and Alice raced up the stairs as the cook yelled after them.

"Come back here, you lazy good-for-nothings!"

They didn't stop until they exited into the bright sunshine. Then they leaned against the Castle wall, panting and laughing.

"She's just upset because she hasn't scrubbed a floor herself in twenty years," Alice said. Then her face grew serious. "I'm glad to be out of there, but you had better not be fooling me, Simon Cobb. I may hate slaving away in that place, but I need that job."

"I'm telling the truth, I swear," Simon replied, recounting everything that had happened since he first stepped into the throne room.

Alice shook her head. "That's pretty brilliant, Simon. At least we have an excuse to stay out of work for a while. But what if we don't find the Princess? I doubt Mary will let me go back to work."

"We can't think like that," Simon said. "I honestly

believe we can do this. We just need to find a way to get to outer space. The Queen seemed to think there might be something that could help us in Mordred's lab, but I don't know how to get there."

Alice frowned, thinking. "I bet those creepy followers of Mordred know how. But they're supersecretive." Then her face lit up. "Hey, I bet we could find out more over at the mill. Nobody there can keep a secret."

"Good idea," Simon said with a nod. "Rose, the lady-in-waiting, mentioned a secret society, too. Not that I'm anxious to meet them or anything, but I think it's our best bet right now."

They headed to the windmill, past the Castle and the stables, climbing over haystacks along the way. Simon felt bold and full of adventure, but as they approached the windmill entrance and the sound of chatting voices floated out, he suddenly grew shy.

"You go in first," he said, nodding to Alice.

Alice shook her red curls. "Honestly, Simon, they're not going to bite."

Simon shrugged. "I'm used to horses. People, not so much."

Alice pulled him by the arm. "They're harmless. You'll see."

Inside, the mill was cool and dim. About a dozen teenagers from the village were hanging out there. The young girls wore flower crowns with dresses to match, and the boys wore simple peasant shirts, trousers, and scuffed leather shoes.

A bucktoothed boy waved to Alice. "Hey there, Allie! What's up?"

Simon turned to her. "Allie?"

Alice shrugged. "I hang out here sometimes. No big deal." She approached the boy. "So, Garth, what's new?"

"I heard that Sir Gawain wears green underwear," Garth reported.

Simon rolled his eyes. "Seriously? This is not helpful at all," he complained.

Another boy with an acne-pocked face sidled right up to them. "I know some good stuff," he said. "For example, I heard that the king and queen are keeping one of the invaders locked in the dungeon."

Alice leaned into Simon. "That's a pretty interesting clue," she whispered.

"How, exactly?" Simon asked, frustrated. "Listen, you talk to these people. I'll be hanging around in the rafters."

"Fine," Alice said, turning back to the gossips.

When he was a young boy, Simon learned to climb the windmill rafters. It was peaceful up there, away from the stench of manure and Tobias's off-key singing and Edmund's yelling. He hoisted himself onto a wooden shelf, and then climbed to the loft just above. The shelves on the wall of the windmill were perfect for jumping to the top of the structure. Then he jumped to the third floor, which held all the giant gears that turned the blades of the windmill. There was a rope hanging from one of the gears, and Simon jumped up to grab it.

Creeeeaaaaaak! The gears slowly began to turn.

"Uh-oh!" Simon said, and he jumped back down to the second level. To his surprise, he found himself face-to-face with a peasant girl. She had black hair, a long black dress, and a belt with a skull. A star necklace dangled from her neck.

The girl eyed Simon.

"Tell me your secret, and I'll tell you mine."

Her voice was like a creaking door in a haunted house, and Simon felt a chill run through his body. But he had come here to learn about the secret society, and the star around her neck reminded Simon of the designs on the fountain. He decided to play along.

"I have this secret message," Simon said, handing

it to the dark-haired girl. "It's from the Princess."

The girl studied the message. "I can see you are a member of the order," she said after a moment. "Here's the password for the entrance."

She slipped a piece of paper into Simon's hand. There were three symbols drawn on it: a moon, a ringed planet, and a star.

The order! The password! This is just what we need! Simon thought, trying to contain his excitement. He coolly slipped the paper into his pocket.

"Thanks," he said. Then he quickly jumped to the first floor. He found Alice and grabbed her by the arm.

"Come on," he said. "I found out something good."

"What is it?" Alice asked eagerly once they were outside.

Simon showed her the paper with the symbols. "This spooky-looking girl gave it to me. She said it's the password to the order."

Alice gasped. "The secret order! Now we have a way in. But where is it?"

"I've been thinking," Simon said carefully. "These look like the symbols on the fountain. And remember when we saw those people in the purple robes? They disappeared near the fountain."

"A secret entrance! Of course!" Alice cried. "Let's go!"

The sun was quickly slipping below the horizon as they made their way to the town square, and a cold chill began to creep into the air.

"I miss the bright lights," Alice said wistfully. "And I forgot to bring a candle with me."

"We're almost there," Simon assured her.

When they got to the fountain, they both jumped in. Simon took out the paper with the code again.

"So do we say the password out loud or something?" Simon guessed. "Moon, planet, star?"

He paused, waiting for something to happen, but the only response was the chirp of a cricket.

"Let's try pressing them," Alice said. She pressed on the moon, and the symbol receded into the stone. "Hey, it's working!"

She pressed the planet, then the star, and they both receded into the plaque. Excited, they waited for some kind of door to open or to get some kind of message to appear, but nothing happened. Alice frowned.

"I guess it's not working after all," she said.

"Maybe there's a final step," Simon suggested. "Try pressing that big sun in the center next."

Alice obeyed, and the sun receded into the stone. Then the whole plaque slid up, revealing a dark hole in the fountain's base. She peered into the chasm.

"It looks really dark down there," she said apprehensively.

"I'm starting to get the idea that you're afraid of the dark," Simon remarked.

"Hey, you don't like people, and I don't like the dark," Alice said with a shrug. "We've all got our thing. Besides, I bet there are people down there, too."

Now it was Simon's turn to be worried. "I forgot. That girl gave me the password because she thought I was a member of the order. We're going to have to act like we know stuff."

"I'll do the talking," Alice promised. She took a deep breath. "Let's get this over with."

They shimmied down a rope and found themselves in a dimly lit underground room. Posters of constellations decorated the crumbling walls, and in the center of the space, surrounded by candles, stood a large statue of Mordred.

A small group of people in purple robes were huddled around the statue. When they noticed Simon and Alice, they walked toward them.

"Oh no," Simon whispered to Alice. "They're going to eat our brains or something."

"Relax!" Alice hissed back.

"Welcome, seekers!" said one of the purple-robed people. Simon realized it was the girl from the mill. "Hail Mordred!" she said.

"Um, hail Mordred," Alice said.

"Yeah, what she said," Simon added.

"It won't be long before Mordred returns to Poptropica and brings peace and prosperity," said the dark-haired girl.

A man with a gray beard approached them. "The King and Queen say that Mordred perished in space, but we know that he lives."

"One of our members has made contact with him,

but we cannot tell you her identity," added a red-haired guy.

Does he mean the Princess? Simon wondered. Rose had secretly been delivering messages from her to the order. He nudged Alice. They needed more information.

Alice gazed around at the creepy decorations. "So, you know, my friend and I are new to this whole secret-order thing. It looks like you've got a lot of, er . . . exciting stuff happening."

"We believe that Mordred was hiding something on top of the windmill," answered a kind-looking old woman. "We're going to investigate tomorrow night when the moon is full! You must join us."

The redheaded boy walked over to a small wood table. "We found this Key in Mordred's house, but we don't know what it goes to," he said, holding it up.

"That's very interesting," Alice said, walking toward him. "Can I see it?"

As Alice examined the Key, the old woman took Simon by the hand. "You two need to get fitted for your robes."

"We, uh, we already have them," Simon lied nervously. "They're at the tailor's. Right, Alice?"

Alice spun around. "Yes, the tailor," she said,

smiling at the old woman. "So we'll just go get them and meet you later, okay?"

The woman nodded. "Hail Mordred!"

They quickly climbed back up the rope and emerged onto the fountain.

"Whoa, those guys were weird," Simon said with a shiver. "But you were great with them. Thanks to you, they gave us an awesome clue about the windmill."

"That's not all they gave us," Alice said, holding up the Key.

Simon grinned. "Awesome."

Alice shrugged. "My dad was a thief. Every once in a while, those skills come in useful."

Simon looked up at the black sky. The moon, just a sliver away from being full, lit up the path ahead of them.

"It's late," he said, "and we need to get up early. We've got to get back to the windmill before they do!"

Chapter Eight

Into the Dungeon

"Rise and shine, sleepyhead!"

Alice opened the door to Simon's hut, expecting him to be snoring in bed. Instead, she found him scrubbed clean and wide awake.

"I'm already up!" he said cheerfully.

Alice pretended to look confused. "I'm sorry, I'm looking for my friend Simon. You know, the guy who never wants to get out of bed in the morning?"

"There's no reason to get out of bed when all you have to look forward to is horse poop," Simon said. "But now we've got a Princess to rescue. Let's get to the windmill!"

Alice slapped a hand to her forehead. "I packed us some food and left it in the Castle kitchen. Let's grab it first. I'm no good at adventuring on an empty stomach."

When they got to the Castle, they saw a villager walking down the front steps, clutching a book. Something clicked in Simon's head.

"Alice, do you still have that library slip we got from the museum?" he asked.

Alice patted her skirt pocket. "Got it right here. I don't leave anything valuable down in the servants' quarters."

"Can I see it for a second?"

"Sure," Alice replied, carefully unfolding the slip and handing it to him.

Simon examined the slip. It was for a book called *Secrets of the Castle: The Shadowy World Beneath Your Feet*. The call number on top read NON-FIC McM. Mordred had taken out the book five times.

"There's got to be a reason that Mordred kept taking out this book," he remarked thoughtfully. "Maybe we should take a look at it."

"What about the windmill?" Alice asked.

"Those weirdos won't make a move until the moon is full," Simon reminded her. "We've got all day. Come on."

They entered the Castle and went to the library on the first floor. The once-grand room had been hit hard during the attack. Books spilled off broken wood shelves, and the stone floor was strewn with stray pages.

"What a shame," Alice said, gazing around with

a sad expression. "This was always my favorite place to sneak off to when Mary wasn't looking. There are some great books in here. I love the books about Mordred's inventions or amazing tales about mystical creatures."

Simon picked up a book from the floor. "Hey, this is interesting. It's called *The Life of Mordred: A Cautionary Tale*. I wonder if any of his secrets are in it."

"We might as well look through it," Alice said.

Simon flipped through the pages as they read. "This basically tells us what we already know. Mordred was an inventor who did good things for the kingdom. Then he started to make dark things, so the King put him in prison. But Mordred kept making inventions in a secret bunker. When the Royal Guard discovered it, Mordred escaped in a rocket ship."

They examined the pictures of Mordred, who had a pointy beard and wore a jacket that was half purple, half orange, and a purple cap with an orange feather in it.

"Is that an owl?" Alice asked, pointing to one of the pictures. "It's strange looking, isn't it? Like it's made of metal."

Simon thought of the mouse he had seen in Rose's room. "Mordred was definitely up to some strange things. But there's nothing in here about how he got into space. We should probably find the book we came here for."

They followed the call letters engraved into small bronze plaques on the shelves until they found what they were looking for: NON-FIC McM.

Simon took the book off the shelf and started to flip through it.

"I don't see what's so special about it," he said.

"Maybe we need to read the whole thing," Alice said thoughtfully.
"It might be written in code. Like where the first letter of each paragraph spells out a message if you put them together."

She took the book from Simon and started studying it. Bored, Simon's glance drifted to the shelf the book had sat on. A strange round knob protruded from the stone wall behind it.

"What's this?" he wondered out loud. Curious, he touched the knob.

To his amazement, a stone door in the floor slid

open right at their feet! He nudged Alice. "Look!"

She peered down at the floor. "It's a secret entrance!"

"Maybe it leads to Mordred's secret bunker, like it says in *The Life of Mordred*," Simon said, getting excited. "There may be a flying craft down there!"

He hurried down the dark staircase, followed by Alice, and they ended up in an underground dungeon. One candle burned on the wall, casting dim light in the space. A loaf of dry bread and hunk of moldy cheese sat on a rickety table.

"Looks like the dungeon keeper's lunch," Alice mused, stepping toward the table. "But there hasn't been a prisoner here since—aaaah!"

She screamed and jumped back, nearly knocking down Simon.

"What's wrong?" he asked, steadying himself.

Trembling, Alice pointed toward the bars of the dungeon cell. Simon's eyes widened as a strange creature emerged from the shadows and floated over the stone floor, hovering behind the bars.

The mechanical creature had a big, glowing yellow eye and a shining green dome on top of its head. Its body was shaped like a metal box, and it had no legs, just two long, blue arms.

"What is that thing?" Alice asked.

"I don't know," Simon replied. "But I bet Mordred made it."

Now that the shock had passed, Alice became more curious. She slowly moved closer to the bars. "I wonder what it does."

"Maybe it can build us a ship to the stars," Simon said hopefully. He pulled on the bars. "But I guess we'll never know for sure. There's no way in there."

Alice nodded to a lever on the wall. "Maybe this opens it."

She pulled the lever, but the cell door didn't open. Instead, a small door inside the cell opened up. Simon frowned.

"That's strange," he said. "I wonder what's on the other side."

Alice looked thoughtful. "You know, the Castle servants were always whispering about some secret lab that Mordred had built when he was in prison. They say that's how he escaped—he built something that could blast through stone. I was never sure if it was true. But now . . ."

"There must be a way to get to the other side," Simon mused. "Maybe we should explore the Castle while we're here. See if we can find that lab."

"Good idea," Alice agreed.

Before they headed out, Simon grabbed the moldy cheese from the table. Alice looked at him quizzically.

"I told you that I've got lunch for us downstairs," she said.

"It's not for us," he replied. "Just something I need to take care of."

When they went back upstairs, they were greeted by the monk who oversaw the library—and two armed Castle guards.

"You shouldn't be snooping around down there," the monk scolded them.

"But we're on a mission for the King!" Simon protested. "We're trying to find the Princess, and to do that we need to see if Mordred—"

"The King has forbidden anyone to utter that name in this Castle!" the monk said sternly. "Now leave, or I will have the guards escort you out."

"Dusty old crank," Alice muttered under her breath as they left.

"Now I'm more convinced than ever that there's some kind of secret lab down there," Simon said. "Why else would they be guarding it?"

"Let's go to the kitchen," Alice suggested. "Nobody will notice if we snoop around there."

"Good idea. But there's something I want to do first," he said.

Alice followed Simon down the hall to Rose's room, where he stopped and knocked on the door.

"Come in!"

They entered and found Rose at her dressing table, sobbing.

"What's wrong?" Simon asked.

"I just miss Elyana so much," the lady-in-waiting said through her tears. "I know I'm just her servant, but we were best friends. I'm so worried about her. I wanted to go to her room and get a kerchief or a trinket—something to remember her by, but the King still has the room locked tight."

"I'm sorry," Simon said sincerely. "I can't help you with that, but I think I can help you with another problem."

He took the moldy cheese from his pocket and placed it on the floor.

"Here, mousie mousie!"

The mechanical mouse emerged from under Rose's dresser, rolled toward the cheese, and began to sniff. Simon reached down and picked it up.

"Got it!" he cried triumphantly.

Alice ran and grabbed a cloth sack from Rose's

dresser. "Put it in here so it doesn't get away."

Simon obeyed, and Alice curiously peered into the sack.

"Did Mordred make this?" she asked.

Rose nodded. "One of his dreadful creatures. Thank you for capturing it for me."

She leaned down and kissed Simon on the forehead. He blushed.

"It's no big deal," he said shyly.

Alice looked annoyed. "Come on," she said, grabbing his arm. "We've got a Castle to explore!"

Chapter Nine

Elyana's Secret

Simon waved good-bye to Rose as he and Alice left the room.

"Can I hold the mouse?" Alice asked. "I still can't believe that Mordred made it."

"It's all yours," Simon said, handing it to her. Alice tied the sack to the belt around her waist, and they made their way to the servants' quarters. Alice grabbed the lunch she'd left behind, and they searched the downstairs hallways, looking for some kind of secret entrance—with no luck.

"I guess it's no use," Alice said with a sigh.

"We need more information," Simon said. "I keep wondering what the Princess has to do with all this. I wish we could get into her room."

"Well, there's a door on her balcony," Alice said. "But we'd have to climb up."

"I can climb!" Simon said. "Let's check it out!"

They went outside and gazed up at the Castle turrets. Alice pointed to a door on one of them.

"That's it," she said, "but I don't know. The walls of the Castle are pretty smooth."

Simon tried to scale the wall, but he quickly discovered that Alice was right. Frowning, he stepped back and looked up at the tower.

"Maybe if we had a rope or something," he mused.

"I think I saw one over by the mill the other day," Alice said. "Hold on."

She returned moments later, cheeks red, holding a coil of rope.

"Don't know how much good it will do," she said. "There's nothing for it to latch on to up there."

Simon swung the rope like a lasso and launched it into the air. It smacked against the balcony and then plummeted, landing at Simon's feet.

"There's got to be a way," Simon said stubbornly. He launched the rope again, but once again it failed to latch on to the balcony.

As the rope sank back down to the ground, Simon noticed the crossbow on the platform above the Castle entrance. He remembered how Sir Cador had used it to take down the flying machines . . . and then he got an idea.

Simon picked up the rope and began to climb onto the platform.

"Where are you going?" Alice called up.

Too excited to answer, Simon quickly tied the rope to the end of one of the long, heavy arrows. Then he tied the other end to the bottom arm of the crossbow to anchor it. The crossbow was attached to a large wheel that could be turned to aim the arrow. He turned the wheel so that the arrow was pointing right at the door in the tower.

Alice climbed onto the platform. "Oh, I get it," she said. "You're going to shoot the arrow into the door, right?"

"Exactly," Simon said confidently.

Then he pulled the lever on the crossbow, and the arrow shot through the air. But it missed its mark, falling to the ground below.

"Rats!" Simon complained, pulling up the rope.

"Maybe you need to adjust the wheel," Alice suggested. She stepped in front of him and placed the arrow back in the crossbow. Then she turned the wheel so that the arrow was aimed a little higher.

"Looks good," Simon agreed. He pulled the arrow back a second time.

Ziiing! The arrow whizzed through the air and landed securely in the wood door. Now the rope stretched from the Castle right to the tower. Perfect!

"Huzzah!" Simon cheered. He walked over to the rope and pulled himself on top. "I'll search her room and try to find out the connection between her and that secret order."

He slowly stood up on the rope, balancing. Then he took one careful step after another, trying to keep his balance like a circus performer. When he reached the mysterious door, he pushed it open and jumped inside.

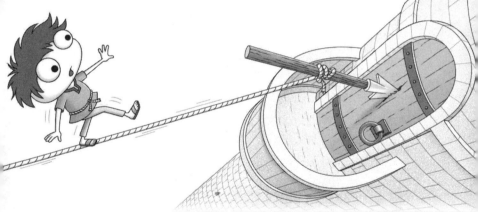

The Princess's room contained a pink carpet, a pink bed, and a dresser with a crown carved into the mirror. The invaders' bombs had left the place a wreck, just as they had the rest of the Castle. There were tattered posters of stars and planets on the walls, just like the ones he and Alice had seen in the order's secret hideout.

Simon wasn't exactly sure what he was looking for, but he figured he would know when he saw it. There was a bunch of jewelry, a hairbrush, and some fancy clothes in the dresser.

Then he opened up a wood chest at the foot of the Princess's bed. Inside, he found an interesting scrap of paper that had been damaged by the attack. A smile spread across his face as he read it.

"Wait until Alice sees this," Simon said. He tucked it into his pocket and made his way back outside, across the rope, and then jumped down to the platform.

"Thank goodness! I kept imagining you falling off the rope," Alice said with relief.

"Gosh, nice imagination," Simon said sarcastically. He handed her the scrap of paper. "Anyway, I found something. Read this."

The order believes the Great Inventor kept many of his secrets under his bed, but the order dare not come out of its hiding place to seek them. I will do my best to aid them in their search because I believe Mordred is alive! I've detected a beacon on a faraway planet, and I believe it must have been sent from him. I have sent a return signal and . . .

Alice's eyes grew wide. "It sounds like the Princess liked Mordred . . . you know, *liked* him."

"Gross," Simon said, making a face. "But I thought the King said Mordred was all evil and stuff. Why would the Princess like him?"

Alice sighed. "It's a girl thing. You wouldn't understand. But, anyway, this proves that Mordred really *did* escape to outer space, and the Princess was contact with him."

Simon was more confused than ever. "Okay. So Mordred escaped to a faraway planet. Someone from outer space kidnapped the Princess. But if Mordred and the Princess were friends, why would he kidnap her?"

"Maybe he didn't kidnap her," Alice replied. "Maybe he rescued her."

"Rescued her?" Simon asked.

"From her strict parents," Alice said, getting a dreamy look in her eyes. "It's so romantic! For years, Princess Elyana searched the skies, waiting for her true love to return. Then one day, Mordred swooped down from the heavens and swept her away."

"After blowing up a bunch of stuff," Simon pointed out. "So if that's true, wouldn't the knights have come back and told us that by now? It doesn't make sense."

"Good point," Alice admitted. "I guess there's only one way to find out the truth."

Simon nodded. "That's right. We still need to find a way to get to outer space!"

Chapter Ten

Finally . . . a Flying Machine!

"We should go back to the museum and look under Mordred's bed," Alice suggested. "The Princess said he kept secrets under there."

Simon shook his head. "Are you forgetting about the windmill? We've got to get there before the full moon tonight. Let's do that now while we're here."

"You're right," Alice agreed.

They walked over to the windmill, and Simon stopped by the door.

"You know, I climbed up in there the other day," he said. "I didn't find anything of Mordred's. Just that strange girl."

"You mean you were all the way up there?" Alice asked, pointing to the top of the mill, which was covered by a round glass dome.

Simon frowned. "I didn't see a dome above me," he said. "That means there must be a secret room under there!"

"Mordred's secret room," Alice reminded him.

"We've got to get up there and check it out," Simon said eagerly. He hopped on the nearest large windmill blade, and the blades slowly began to spin, lifting him a few feet off the ground.

"Excellent! We can ride the blades to the top!" Alice said, her eyes shining with excitement. She eagerly jumped onto the blade with Simon—a little too eagerly. The windmill groaned as the blades quickly made another counterclockwise turn, and Alice almost lost her balance.

"Whoa!" Alice cried, steadying herself.

She and Simon jumped to the next blade, and the windmill turned again.

"Hey, look up there!" Simon cried when they were about halfway up. The glass dome was now about halfway open on its hinges. "I think it opens a little every time the blades turn."

Simon climbed up to the next blade, keeping watch on the dome. Just as he had guessed, it opened a little bit more. By the time Simon reached the top, the dome was open all the way.

He peered down inside but couldn't see anything except a dusty wood floor. He was eager to jump down but wanted to be fair to Alice.

69

"We made it!" Alice cheered. "Now let's see what's in that secret room."

Whomp! They both jumped down, landing safely in a soft stack of hay.

Alice leaped up, brushing hay off her dress.

"It doesn't look like we'll find anything up here except maybe some mice," she said, gazing around. Then she patted the sack hanging from her belt. "No offense, Mordred Mouse."

Simon started to look around. "There must be something hidden, maybe under a board in the floor," he suggested. "Or inside a—ow!"

"What's an *ow*?" Alice teased.

"There's something hard under here," Simon said, kicking the haystack he'd just bumped into.

He began to push aside the hay, and Alice joined him. They quickly revealed what was hidden underneath—a shiny metal craft!

"This must be what the secret order was talking about," Simon guessed.

"Do you think it's a spaceship?" Alice asked.

Simon walked around the craft. It was smaller than the ones that had come from the sky, and there was no glass dome on the top.

"I'm not sure," he said, and then he jumped into

the pilot's seat. "But there's only one way to find out."

Alice hesitated just a second before jumping in beside him. "Might as well. The more time I spend out of that kitchen, the more I don't want to go back."

"All right. Brace yourself," Simon said, and Alice closed her eyes and gripped the side of the craft. Then Simon pressed the green button marked START on the control panel in front of him . . . and nothing happened.

Alice opened her eyes. "What's wrong?"

"I'm not sure," Simon said.

Alice pointed to a gauge on the panel that read FUEL. The arrow was pointing to EMPTY.

"I guess it needs fuel to run," Alice said. "But what kind?"

Simon climbed out of the craft and walked around it. "It looks like this is where the fuel goes," he said. He unscrewed the cap and peered into the hole.

"Phew! I'd know that smell anywhere. This thing runs on manure," Simon said.

Alice grinned. "Lucky us! There's plenty of that around here."

"Don't I know it," Simon grumbled. "Be right back."

He climbed out of the windmill and returned a few

minutes later carrying a sack of manure. Holding his nose, he dumped it into the fuel tank. Then he jumped back into the craft.

"This better work," he said, pressing START once more.

This time, the craft roared to life. It quickly shot straight up into the air through the top of the windmill.

"We're going to the stars!" Alice shrieked, laughing.

The craft lurched wildly from side to side. Simon started pressing buttons like crazy until the craft evened out.

"I don't know," Simon said. "I don't think it goes much higher. But I think we can go lower. See?"

He pulled on a stick coming out of the control panel, and the craft gently lowered until it was hovering just a few feet off the ground.

"Whoo! This is almost better than riding a horse!" Simon cried as the craft zipped across the muddy field next to the windmill.

Alice's eyes were shining. "This is fun! Can it go faster?"

Simon tried some more buttons, but the speed didn't change.

"I guess not," he said. "This thing is cool, but I

don't think it will get us into space."

"It might not," Alice agreed. "But *that* might."

She pointed to an object sticking out of the mud in the middle of the field. It was another spacecraft— larger than the little landskimmer they had found and with a clear dome on top.

"It's one of the invaders' ships!" Simon said excitedly. He pulled back on the control stick, and the landskimmer hovered right next to the craft. Simon jumped out.

"Does it work?" Alice asked.

Simon opened the dome and climbed into the cockpit. "The panel here says that the fuel is empty, too," he said.

"We should get more manure," Alice suggested.

"There's plenty of it around here."

"Don't I know it," Simon muttered. He climbed out of the cockpit and examined the craft. The word *Excalibur* was painted on the side. Simon kept searching but couldn't find the fuel tank.

"I don't see a fuel tank like the one on the landskimmer," he reported. "I don't think this thing uses manure."

Alice frowned. "Too bad we don't have any *space* manure," she said. "Maybe that would do the trick."

Simon thought for a minute. "Wait a second. When Mordred escaped from the dungeon, he flew into space, right? So he must have used something from around here."

Alice nodded. "I bet the secret is in his lab. I just wish we could find it!"

Chapter Eleven

The Secret under the Hay

Simon and Alice hopped into the landskimmer and sped across the muddy field.

"We'd better hide this thing," Alice suggested. "We don't want the secret order to find it."

They quickly hid it under a pile of hay and then sat down with their backs against it. Alice took a flask of water from her pouch, took a sip, and handed it to Simon.

"Looks like we're stuck," she said.

Simon shook his head. "We can't be. There's got to be something we're forgetting. Let's try to think back over the last day."

"Well, let's see," Alice began. "The lady-in-waiting told us that she was delivering secret messages to the order for the Princess. Then you got into the Princess's room and found out that she was a member of the order and she was in touch with Mordred."

Simon nodded. "And the secret order told us there

was something in the windmill, which we found."

They were both quiet for a moment, thinking.

"Wait a second," Alice said finally. "Didn't the Princess say some other things in her letter?"

Simon took the crumpled paper from his pocket. "Here it is," he said. He began to read aloud. "'The order believes the Great Inventor kept many of his secrets under his bed, but the—'"

"That's it!" Alice cried. "She must be talking about his bed—the one in the museum. Maybe there's a map to the location of his secret lab or something!"

Simon's eyes brightened. "It's worth a try. Let's go see what we can find."

They hurried back to town and ran into the museum. The curator coughed politely.

"You need one coin—"

"We're on official business from the King!" Alice announced as she and Simon breezed past him. The curator didn't know what to make of that, so he let them pass. They climbed up the rickety stairs and knelt down in front of Mordred's old bed.

Alice slid underneath, pushing away cobwebs. Then she triumphantly emerged holding a yellowed piece of paper.

"I found something!" she cried, holding up a yellowed piece of paper. Simon leaned in to read it.

I have found a nearby moon with activity that I believe to be alien life! I have found that animal waste makes decent fuel, and there is just enough manure in Arturus to bring my flying craft to this moon. The star coordinates are x-56, y-52.

"'Alien life?'" Simon asked.

"It means . . . from another place," Alice said. "He means that he found people—or something—living on this moon."

"Maybe those aliens are the ones who attacked us," Simon guessed. "Anyway, this isn't much help. Mordred says he used manure to take his craft to the moon, but I don't see how I'm supposed to get manure into that ship we found in the mud."

"Maybe he did something to change the manure," Alice mused. "You know, to make it work in the flying craft."

"Which is exactly why we need to find his lab," Simon pointed out. "Isn't there anything else under there? Like a map?"

Alice shook her head, stood up, and dusted her hands off on her skirt. "Nothing except for dust bunnies and cobwebs. But you're welcome to look yourself."

Simon stood up. "Forget it." He said. Then he marched downstairs without saying another word.

Alice followed him outside. "We can't give up now!" she urged.

"It doesn't matter," Simon said. "I don't know what I was thinking, anyway. I'm just a stable boy. Did I really think I could fly to the stars and rescue the Princess?"

"Yes, you did," Alice reminded him. "And you can. *We* can."

They walked past the Planetarium and the Crop Circle Inn and headed for the Castle. Two large haystacks sat on the path in front of them.

"More hay!" Simon complained. "Did Mordred know a way to turn hay and manure into gold? Because that would actually have been useful in a place like this."

He gave the haystack a good kick, and the bundle nudged forward. To his surprise, Simon saw a gleam of metal on the ground by the stack.

"What's this?" he wondered. Curious, he gave the stack a push, groaning, until he revealed a round, wooden door with metal hinges.

"Now that's interesting," Alice remarked.

"It looks like it goes underground," Simon said, kneeling down. Then he frowned. "But there's a lock on it."

Alice reached into her pocket. "Maybe this will work," she said, handing him a Key. "It's the one I swiped from the order, remember?"

Simon grinned. "Alice, you are the best!" he said, and his friend blushed. Simon took the Key, opened the lock, and slowly opened the door. A rope dangled down into a dark hole.

A mechanical whirring sound came from down in the hole. Simon and Alice peered down, and they saw two blue, glowing eyes coming up through the darkness—fast.

"Look out!" Alice warned.

They quickly darted out of the way as a winged creature flew out of the hole into the light. Its entire body—sharp claws, pointy beak, wings, and feathers— was made of metal.

"It's Mordred's mechanical owl!" Simon cried.

Chapter Twelve

Inside Mordred's Dungeon

The owl flew in circles, blocking their way into the underground passage.

Alice was fascinated. "It's like, part owl, part . . . something else. In those books about Mordred I read, he called his mechanical creatures 'robots.'"

Inside the pouch hanging from her waist, the robot mouse began to wiggle and squeak.

"It can probably sense the owl," Simon guessed. "I saw a barn owl swoop down and grab a mouse once in the stables. I couldn't believe how fast it moved!"

Alice thoughtfully looked down at the pouch. "It might work," she mumbled. "But it's too cruel."

Simon suddenly realized what she meant. "Of course! Maybe if we feed the mouse to the owl it will let us pass."

Alice hugged the pouch. "But it's just an innocent little mouse!"

"It's not a real mouse," Simon reminded her. "It's a robot. Mordred created it. And right now it's our best chance of finding out what's at the end of that rope."

Alice sighed and nodded. "You're right," she said, opening the pouch. She took out the mouse and placed it on the ground. "Good-bye, Mordred Mouse."

Before the robot mouse could skitter away, the robot owl eagerly swooped down and ate it in one gulp. Then it flew to Alice and hovered next to her shoulder.

"I think it likes you," Simon remarked.

"It's amazing," Alice said, studying the tiny metal gears and parts that made up its body. "Mordred must have been a real genius."

"More like an *evil* genius," Simon said. "At least, that's what it sounds like. But we'll never know unless we find that secret bunker of his. Let's go!"

Simon shimmied down the rope, and Alice followed with the owl flapping his wings behind her. They jumped down into what looked like an underground lab. The wall was covered with plans for a spaceship, the robot owl, and the robot mouse. A portrait of Mordred hung crookedly over a desk strewn with papers. Gears and tools littered a rickety wood table.

"We found it!" Simon cried excitedly. "Mordred's

secret bunker! There's got to be something in here that tells us how to get that flying craft going."

Alice picked up a leather-bound journal from the desk.

"Maybe it's in here," she said. She and Simon began to read the pages.

I've begun doing experiments of a very different kind. I've found that by mixing animal DNA and robotics, I can create a whole new breed of intelligent creatures. I've created a companion whom I shall call Merlin. Part barn owl and part machine. I believe I've made a breakthrough for the ages.

Alice looked up from the page and smiled at the owl. "Oh, hello, Merlin." Then they read the next entry.

I've been ordered by the King and Queen to stop my experimentation. Curse them for their unenlightened thinking! It has been many months since I last wrote. I was jailed by the King and Queen, and it took me a great long while to tunnel out. But now I have returned to the lab, where I will continue my work.

"So this *is* his secret lab," Simon remarked.

Failure! I have ambitious designs, but they require more power than this world can provide.

"Hmm," Simon mused. "Sounds like he discovered that the manure wasn't enough to power his spaceship. But he must have found something. After all, he made it to spacc in the end."

Then they read the very last entry.

They are coming! I must escape to the stars, even though my experimental craft is not ready. I fear I shall not survive!

"Okay," Simon said, closing the book. "So it looks like we need to find a different kind of fuel if we want to power that spaceship. It's got to be in here somewhere. Or at least instructions on how to make it."

Simon and Alice tore apart the lab, looking for anything they could find about the fuel. But they couldn't find a thing.

"Rats!" Simon said, kicking the dirt wall behind him. "We are never going to get into space!"

Alice was looking at the wall thoughtfully. "Hold on a second," she said. "Let's think this through. The king put Mordred in a dungeon. Mordred dug a tunnel into this room and made it his secret lab. After Mordred escaped, the King must have blocked the tunnel. There might be something important in there."

"Hey, that's not a bad idea!" Simon said. He kicked the wall again. "It should be just behind this, right?"

Dirt crumbled and flew into the air as Simon kicked it again. Alice joined him, and soon they had kicked a hole through the dirt that blocked the tunnel.

"There's *got* to be something good in here," Simon said hopefully. He took off running into the tunnel, and Alice and Merlin followed him. The tunnel ended at a low opening in the wall shaped like a half circle. They ducked and went through the opening—and found themselves in the dungeon cell with the weird, one-eyed robot!

"*Aaaaaaaaah!*" Simon and Alice screamed.

"INTRUSION. SELF DESTRUCT," the robot said.

The dome on top of the robot's head opened up,

and a glowing green rod flew out and landed outside
the bars of the cell. Then the robot's green eye went
dark, and it collapsed to the floor in a heap of metal.

Alice sighed with relief. "Thank goodness. Merlin
here is beautiful, but that . . . thing is just too creepy."

Simon walked to the bars and looked out. "You
know, that green rod seemed to be powering that
robot. I wonder if it could power up the flying craft for
us. It looks like it's the right size and shape."

Alice walked next to him. "I think you're right!"

Excited, Simon thrust his arm between the bars, but he couldn't reach it. "Rats! I can't get it. And if we try to get to the dungeon from the other side, the guards will stop us."

Alice tried to squeeze through the bars. "It's impossible," she said. Then she eyed the robot owl. "But not for Merlin. Do you think he would listen to us?"

Simon shrugged. "Why not? Give it a try."

Alice looked up at the metal bird and smiled

sweetly. "Hey, Merlin, can you please fetch us that fuel rod?"

Without hesitating, Merlin flapped his wings, flew through the bars, and picked up the fuel rod in his talons. Then he flew back through the bars and dropped the rod into Alice's hands.

"Thanks, Merlin," Alice said, patting him on the head.

Simon grinned. "If this works in the flying craft, we can finally rescue the Princess!"

Chapter Thirteen

Beyond the Fabric of the Sky

Simon and Alice climbed back out of Mordred's secret lab. Merlin followed them as they retrieved the landskimmer from its hiding place in the hay and then zoomed across the muddy field, back to the flying craft.

Simon pulled back the control stick, and the landskimmer hovered in midair. They cautiously climbed out and entered the flying craft. Simon took out the green glowing rod and examined the control panel inside the cockpit. The rod fit perfectly into a slot on the panel. The *Excalibur* began to hum to life, and the control panel lit up.

Simon let out a cheer. "Huzzah! It works! Now we can go rescue the Princess!"

"We're forgetting something," Alice reminded him. "The Princess liked Mordred. What if she doesn't want to be rescued?"

"We need to find out for sure," Simon reasoned.

"And besides, the knights are missing, too. I have a feeling that there's trouble up there."

Alice squeezed in next to him inside the cockpit.

"Come on, Merlin," she said, coaxing the owl closer. "I don't think you can fly as high as we're going."

Merlin swooped into the cockpit and sat on Alice's shoulder. Simon lowered the dome over them and settled in the pilot's chair.

"All right," he said. "We should probably head to that moon Mordred talked about in that page we found under his bed."

Alice fished the paper from her pocket and read from it. "Mordred says that the star coordinates for the moon with alien life are X-56, Y-52."

They studied the control panel. "I think we just push in the numbers here, right?"

He entered the numbers and turned to Alice. "You know, this is a big risk. What if something happens to this craft? We might never be able to get back here."

Alice shrugged. "I don't think I'd miss it too much. Would you?"

"No, I guess not," Simon admitted. "Except for the horses, maybe."

He took a deep breath and pressed the button

marked LAUNCH. The spaceship began to rumble and shake, and then suddenly . . .

Whoosh! The ship shot out of the mud and zoomed into the sky. The ship was whizzing past the clouds in the blue sky so fast they were just a blur. Below, they could see the islands of Poptropica floating in the blue water.

"Huzzah! Now *this* is fun!" Alice cheered.

Then they entered the blackness of space, and the blurry clouds gave way to blurry stars. In the distance, they could see a bumpy moon the color of dull metal.

"That must be where we're going," Alice reasoned.

"Mordred said there was alien life on that moon. I wonder what the aliens look like."

"I never really thought of that," Simon said, suddenly sounding nervous. "What if they're enormous? With pointy teeth and sharp claws?"

"We won't know until we get there," Alice said matter-of-factly. "And there's no point in worrying about it now. We've got to face whatever's in store for us."

Then a loud beeping sound filled the craft. The lights on the control panel began to blink on and off. A message appeared on the screen.

WARNING. FUEL ROD DEPLETED.

"No fuel?" Simon asked. He glanced at the fuel rod to see that there was only a sliver left of the glowing green fuel. The spacecraft began to wickedly spiral toward the moon's surface.

"Hold on!" Alice yelled. They both closed their eyes as *Excalibur* crashed into the surface of the moon.

Chapter Fourteen

Little Green Aliens

Crash! Everything turned upside down as the ship made contact with the surface of the moon. Lights flashed on and off, and smoke streamed from the control panel.

Simon pushed open the cracked dome and climbed out of the spaceship. He was shaken, but not hurt. Alice looked pale as she climbed out behind him.

"Are you all right?" he asked.

Alice nodded. "I can't believe we're not hurt. If Mordred built that machine, he knew what he was doing."

Then she looked around. "Oh no! Where's Merlin?"

To her relief, the owl flew out of the wreck, circled around them both, and settled on a metal sign that read Welcome to Pewter Moon. The sign was missing a big chunk out of it.

"It looks like whoever attacked Arturus hit this place, too," Simon remarked.

"Everything seems calm now, though," Alice

pointed out. "So we know that this is the moon that Mordred traveled to. I guess we should start looking for him."

"I hope we find him and not some horrible, snarling alien creatures," Simon said with a shudder.

Suddenly, they heard a voice behind them.

"Welcome!"

They both turned around to see a creature wearing a white spacesuit with black trim. He had green skin with light green spots, bushy green hair, and two wiggling green antennae on top of his head.

Simon and Alice might have been frightened if he didn't look so small and cute.

"Excuse me, sir," Simon said politely. "But are you an alien?"

The green man laughed. "I live here, so I guess not. Seems to me that *you're* the alien around here."

He waved and walked away, leaving Simon and Alice just a little bit stunned.

"So this moon must be inhabited by little green people," Alice reasoned. "These must have been here when Mordred landed. We should see if we can find any more of them so we can ask."

"Good idea," Simon said. "But where do we start?"

The two friends took in their surroundings. Luckily, they had crashed right in front of what looked like a space station. Metal towers rose from the surface on spindly legs. They surrounded a large, round metal building that stood about twenty feet off the ground. Right next to them was a strange-looking platform with the words Create Your Own Rocket above it. Next to it flashed a screen that read HOLOPAD CONSOLE.

Alice walked toward it, fascinated. "Do you think Mordred built this?" she said, touching the buttons on the console. "This might come in useful. Now that *Excalibur*'s in pieces, we'll need a way to get home."

An alien wearing a T-shirt with a rocket on it quickly approached her.

"Sorry, no messing around with this unless you talk with my boss," he said in a cranky voice.

"Oh, sorry," Alice said. "Maybe you can help us. Do you know a man named Mordred?"

But the alien just glared at her. He clearly didn't like strangers.

"Come on, Alice," Simon said. "Let's check out the main building."

As they made their way there, a friendlier looking alien walked up to them.

"The head mechanic might be able to fix that ship of yours," she informed them, nodding toward their wrecked ship. "He's inside."

She nodded to the building above them. There were no stairs leading to the top. Instead, a levitating pad traveled slowly from the ground to the building and then back again.

Simon stared at it a moment in wonder. "This is amazing," he said. "Just a few days ago, I was shoveling manure in a stable. And now . . . I'm here. It's like a dream."

"I know," Alice agreed. "This beats scrubbing floors."

The two of them jumped onto the levitating pad, steadying themselves as they landed. Merlin hovered next to Alice, flapping his wings as the pad carried them up to the shop.

When they reached the landing, Simon yelled, "Jump," and they landed safely in front of the shop entrance. A sign above the door read, "Astrozone: For All Your Rocket Needs."

Alice saw an alien pacing up and down the walkway next to the entrance.

"Excuse me, are you the boss?" she asked.

"No," he replied. "I'm keeping an eye out for the Binary Bard. He attacked us once, and he's likely to do it again."

Alice and Simon looked at each other, confused.

"Binary Bard? Who's he?" Simon asked.

"He's a powerful sorcerer who lives across the galaxy," the alien explained. "He wants to steal our technology. Some say he is creating machines to carry out his evil plans."

Simon turned to Alice and said, "So do you think this Binary Bard is the one who attacked Arturus?"

Alice frowned. "I was sure that it was Mordred," she said thoughtfully. "But then again, we don't really know what happened to Mordred once he arrived here. Maybe this Binary Bard captured Mordred and the Princess!"

Simon shook her head. "This is getting pretty confusing. Let's go find that green guy's boss and see if we can fix the *Excalibur*. We can't do anything if our ship doesn't work."

They walked inside Astrozone and found themselves in a bright space with shelves lined with rocket fuel, tools, rocket fins, and other rocket parts. A green alien with a spiky haircut stood next to the door.

"Are you the head mechanic?" Simon asked him.

"Sure am," the alien replied. "Welcome to Astrozone."

"A girl outside said you might be able to fix our ship for us," Alice said.

The alien laughed. "That wreck? Not a chance."

Alice and Simon exchanged worried glances. "Could you lend us one of yours, then, please?" Alice asked.

"No way," the mechanic replied. "The last time I lent a ship to a human I never saw it again."

Simon looked excited. "A human? Was his name Mordred?"

The alien shrugged. "He didn't tell me his name.

Guess I should have asked for it."

"So you've never heard of a Mordred around here?" Alice pressed him.

"Nope," the alien replied. "Sorry."

"Another dead end," Simon said glumly.

"Maybe not," Alice said. "We still have those coordinates the Queen gave us, remember? The ones the knights left her? We can travel to those places and keep looking."

"But we don't have a ship, remember?" Simon said.

Alice turned to the mechanic and flashed him her best smile.

"Please, sir," she said. "We have come such a long way. We're on a rescue mission. The Princess of our kingdom has been taken, and we fear the worst. But we cannot save her if we don't have a ship. Can you please help us?"

The alien's green cheeks blushed as blue as a cornflower. "Tell you what," he said. "Leave me your ship for scrap, and you can build a new one on the holopad."

Alice's face lit up. "Oh, thank you so much! We'll be sure to tell the King and Queen how kind you were to us."

The mechanic blushed again.

"Thanks for your help," Simon added.

They jumped back on the floating pad and got off on the moon's surface. Back at the holopad, the cranky alien nodded to them.

"The boss just buzzed me. If he says it's okay, I guess it's okay," he said.

"So how do you work this thing?" Simon asked, but the unfriendly alien had already wandered off.

Simon shrugged. "Pressing buttons seems to work. Let's try this one."

He was in luck, because the big screen turned on and an image of a basic rocket ship appeared. Simon read the instructions out loud.

"'You can choose what kind of body shape, wings, and door you want,'" he said. "'Just click on each part, and the graphic on the left will show you the balance of speed and shields in each design.'"

"Shields? I guess they must protect the ship," Alice said. "That sounds like a good idea."

"Speed is important, too," Simon countered. "We've wasted enough time already. I want to find the Princess, fast."

"Well, the instructions say we need a balance," Alice reminded him.

"A little faster won't hurt," Simon said. He started clicking the buttons until he came to a rocket with a thin body that tapered to a point, streamlined wings, and a sleek steel door.

"That does look impressive," Alice admitted.

"Now for some color," he said. "How about orange, green, and blue? For the knights?"

Alice nodded. "Nice touch."

Simon hit DONE, and the finished rocket appeared on the rocket pad. Green stripes ran down the blue body, and the door and wings were trimmed in orange.

The cranky alien had wandered back.

"Not bad, for a couple humans," he said, admiring their ship.

"Thanks!" Simon said. He reached in his pocket and took out the coordinates the Queen had given him. "So can I just type these in, and the ship will take me there?"

The alien's eyes grew wide. "You're going *there*? Good luck, then," he said. "If your shields get low, just teleport back here."

"What do you mean, *there*?" Simon asked, but the alien just shook his head and walked away once more.

"That didn't sound too promising," Alice said worriedly.

"Nobody said rescuing the Princess was going to be easy," Simon said. "If there's danger ahead, we'll face it bravely, just like Sir Pelleas, Sir Cador, and Sir Gawain!"

Alice took a deep breath. "You're right," she said with a nod.

Inside the ship, they found a control station with a large screen. Simon switched it on, and a map appeared. In the center was home, and the Pewter Moon was close by. The map showed three other planets: the Jungle Planet, the Ice Planet, and the Fire Planet.

"Where should we go first?" Simon asked.

Alice looked thoughtful. "Well, they all sound a bit dangerous. In the stories I've heard, jungles are dark and filled with snakes and deadly creatures. Fires can burn you. So maybe the Ice Planet?"

Simon clicked on the Ice Planet on the map and read from it. "'The planet is surrounded by dangerous mechanical space sharks. Space sharks are virtually indestructible, but even they cannot withstand the pull of a black hole.'"

Simon turned a little pale. "Space sharks? Don't sharks have lots of big, sharp teeth?"

"So what?" Alice asked boldly. "Do you think Sir

Pelleas cares about space sharks? He eats them for breakfast. I know because I make him his breakfast every day."

That made Simon smile. "You're right. We're not afraid of any space sharks. Ice Planet, here we come!"

Chapter Fifteen

Danger on the Ice Planet

Simon's stomach lurched as the rocket lifted off the holopad and soared into space. Through the window they could see nothing but black sky.

On the screen, the images of planets had disappeared. Instead, a grid of coordinates appeared against a backdrop of black space.

"I guess now is when we can use the coordinates," he said. "It looks like the ones we're closest to are X-73, Y-83."

"They must lead to the Ice Planet," Alice guessed.

Simon steered the rocket while watching the coordinates change on the screen. "All right, now we're at X-73, Y-59. Almost there."

Then a message appeared on the screen: WARNING. APPROACHING BLACK HOLE.

"Black hole? That doesn't sound good," Alice remarked.

"Don't worry. The planet's in the opposite direction," Simon said, steering the rocket away. "Let's see. Y-78, Y-79 . . . there it is!"

Through the ship's window they could see the ice-covered planet. Three gigantic mechanical sharks circled the globe.

"Boy, they sure are big," Simon said with a gulp.

"But you built this rocket to be fast, remember?" Alice said. "Just zip right through them."

Simon gritted his teeth and accelerated the rocket. He tried to steer between the tail of one shark and the head of the next, but there wasn't enough room.

Bam! One of the sharks head-butted them. The screen began to flash.

SHIELDS LOW!

"Steer away!" Alice cried. "We can't take another attack or we'll crash!"

Simon quickly obeyed, leaving the orbit of the Ice Planet. The sharks resumed circling the planet, waiting for the next intruder.

"That was close," Simon said with relief, leaning back in his chair.

Alice frowned. "This is a problem. We can't get past those sharks, especially with our shields so low."

Simon looked thoughtful. "There's got to be some way to get past them. Some kind of strategy."

Alice read the map on the screen again. "The map

says a black hole can destroy them. So if there was a way to get them to the black hole . . ."

"It's risky, but it just might work," Simon said.

"You can do it," Alice told him. "You're pretty good at steering this thing."

Simon grinned. "I'm the only one in the stables who can ride that stallion Blackheart without getting thrown. Compared to that, this is pretty easy."

"Then let's do it!" Alice cheered.

Simon steered the rocket back to the Ice Planet. This time, he approached the mechanical sharks slowly.

"Hello there, giant space sharks with the sharp teeth," he said sweetly. "Try and catch us!"

He slowly steered toward the black hole, and the mechanical sharks began to follow.

"It's working!" Alice cried. "Hurry, before they hit us! Our shields can't take it!"

WARNING. APPROACHING BLACK HOLE.

"Slow down!" Alice yelled. "We'll get sucked in."

"Make up your mind!" Simon yelled back at her. "Should I slow down or hurry up?"

Alice's face was as red as her hair. "I don't know!"

Steadying himself, Simon slowly steered closer and closer to the edge of the swirling vacuum with the sharks right on their tail. Too close, and they'd be pulled in just like the sharks.

Alice bit her lip. "We're so close."

"Almost there . . ." Simon said calmly. He steered right to the edge . . . and at the last second, made a sharp left turn. The ship escaped the black hole—but all three sharks got sucked in!

"You did it!" Alice cheered.

Simon let out a deep breath. "Thank goodness."

He steered the rocket back to the Ice Planet's coordinates and landed the craft on an icy ridge in the middle of a frozen sea.

"It looks pretty cold out there," he remarked, gazing out the window.

"I think I see something up on top of that mountain, just across the water," Alice said, gazing out the window. "We can get across by jumping on those chunks of ice."

Simon nodded. "I hope we find *something* here. It wasn't easy getting rid of those sharks."

Alice turned to Merlin. "You stay here and watch the rocket for us, okay?" The owl replied by blinking its glowing eyes.

Simon and Alice stepped out onto the frozen planet. Alice carefully eyed the ice chunks floating in the water. They each seemed to be floating in one place, not drifting, which was good.

"It's just like the pond in winter," Alice said. "This shouldn't be hard. Come on!"

She jumped to the first ice chunk and was able to keep her balance, so she made another quick leap to the second ice chunk. Simon jumped on next to her.

Alice grinned. "So far, so good," she said. At that moment something jumped out of the water and sailed over her head!

"What was that?" Simon cried.

"It looked like some kind of fish—a robot fish," Alice said in disbelief. "We'll have to watch out for them. They jump high, though, so if we're standing still when they jump over us, we should be fine."

It was a good strategy. Alice and Simon hopped to the next ice chunk and patiently waited to make sure there was no fish lurking under the water. Now they were just one chunk away from the shore. They waited again, and this time, another robot fish sailed over their heads. Then they made a final jump and landed on the icy shore.

"Made it!" Alice cheered. "Now we just have to climb the—whoa!"

A large ball of snow came tumbling down the

mountainside. Alice looked up and saw more giant snowballs rolling down.

"This is definitely *not* like anything back home," Simon remarked.

"Nobody said rescuing the Princess was going to be easy," Alice said, reminding him of his earlier statement. "We'll just have to dodge them."

They quickly made their way up the snowy mountain, jumping from one ledge to another and dodging more big snowballs along the way. When they reached the top, Simon let out a cry.

"Sir Gawain! We found you!"

Sir Gawain's ice-blue armor was dripping with ice crystals. The knight's face was hidden behind his helmet, but his eyes looked shocked to see Alice and Simon.

"The stable boy and the girl who brings me breakfast?" he asked in disbelief. "But how did you get here?"

"It's a long story," Simon replied. "The king sent us to find you—and the Princess, of course. Have you seen her? And where are the other knights?"

The knight's eyes looked sad. "I do not know where my comrades are. We split up so we could search the planets and find the Princess. I crash-landed here weeks ago. I have had nothing to eat but fish, and no hope of escape until I saw you two. I am in your debt."

He bowed his head respectfully to them.

"And no sign of the Princess?" Simon asked.

"A fierce beast lives over that ridge," he said, pointing west. "I fear he is guarding the Princess. But I am too weak to fight him."

Simon felt that jolt of courage once more. "I can fight him!"

"And I'll help you," Alice promised.

The knight handed the crystal Force Shield to Simon. "The shield can protect only one of you."

"Then I'm going," Simon said firmly. "Wait here for me. And if something happens, get back to the rocket and get out of here."

"We're not leaving without you," Alice promised, hugging him. "You're going to succeed. I know it!"

"I hope so," Simon said. He broke away from her and put the crystal around his neck. A soft, glowing orb of light surrounded him.

He walked to the ridge. "Okay, beast. Where are you?"

Beyond the ridge he could see only an endless plain of white snow. Then a strange, rumbling sound echoed off the mountainside. The ground beneath his feet began to shake. A wind whipped up as a giant creature rose up from behind the ridge.

"What is that?" Simon whispered, staring at the beast. It looked like a ferocious tiger made of metal, but it was also a flying machine with a large propeller on top. Stripes marked the beast's body, and three round yellow lights glowed on the side of the craft.

"It's some kind of Tiger Copter!" Alice shouted behind him. She had seen pictures of helicopters in the books in the Castle library.

The Tiger Copter was a terrifying sight, but the shield surrounding him gave Simon confidence.

"I am Simon of the Stables!" he called out bravely. "I have come to rescue Princess Elyana!"

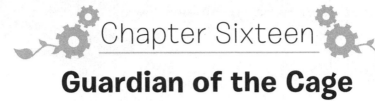

Chapter Sixteen

Guardian of the Cage

The Tiger Copter responded by shooting a barrage of snowballs at Simon. He tried to dodge them, but one hit the shield and bounced right off.

So the shield deflects the snowballs, Simon realized. He wouldn't get hurt as long as the shield held. But how could he do any damage to the copter without a weapon of his own?

Bop! Another snowball hit the shield and bounced off, but this time it hit the Tiger Copter, and one of its yellow lights flickered.

"Of course!" Simon cried. "I can use its own weapons against it!"

Simon kept an eye on the copter so he could try to get into the best position to bounce the snowballs back at the beast.

Bop! Bop! He knocked two snowballs right back at the copter. The beast began to shudder and glow red, and one of the yellow lights went out completely.

"It's working!" Simon cheered. But then he felt the

cold sting of snow on his arm and saw that he'd been hit. The yellow glow of the shield had vanished. His shield was down!

"That didn't last very long," he muttered, complaining. There was nothing to do now but dodge the snowball attack. His feet slipped as he darted across the icy ridge, and he struggled to keep his balance.

What was I thinking? he asked himself as doubt slowly filled his spirit. *How can I fight a huge beast like this by myself? Without even a sword?*

Then he noticed a golden glow rising from his neck and realized that the shield was slowly recharging!

"Hurry, please!" he said.

"Simon! I'm coming to help you!" Alice yelled.

"Stay back!" Simon warned. "I think I've got this!"

Now the shield was fully charged.

Bop! Bop! He bounced two more snowballs at the Tiger Copter, and a second yellow light went out. The beast lurched closer to the mountain, and it looked like it didn't have much longer to last. It weakly hiccuped a snowball in his direction, and Simon easily dodged it.

With his confidence returned, Simon launched his final attack.

Bop! Bop! Bop! Bop! He pummeled the Tiger

Copter with more snowballs. The beast was bright red now, and smoke poured from its nostrils. Something deep inside Simon told him to run away, and he reached safety just as the Tiger Copter crashed into the mountain in a ball of flame.

Simon ran up to the crash and looked over the ridge.

"Princess? Are you there?"

His voice echoed in the mountainside, but there was no response. He couldn't see anything for miles except snow and ice. Alice ran up to him.

"You were amazing!" she said.

"Thanks," Simon replied. "But it was all for nothing. The Princess isn't here."

Alice frowned. "I guess Sir Gawain was wrong," she said. "If you ask me, I think his brain has become frozen out here. He keeps asking me to give him a doughnut."

Frustrated, the friends marched back to Sir Gawain.

"Simon took down the beast," Alice told him. "But we didn't find the Princess."

"Perhaps one of my companions has found her," Sir Gawain replied. "Sir Cador and Sir Pelleas have traveled to other planets in search of the Princess."

"You mean the Jungle Planet and the Fire Planet?" Simon asked.

Sir Gawain nodded. "Yes. I think we should go to your ship at once. I fear my companions need our help."

They made their way back down the mountain and across the icy waters to the rocket. Sir Gawain took off his helmet, and his pale face immediately began to regain color in the warm craft.

"Girl, how about that doughnut?" he asked Alice. "Or perhaps some hot chocolate?"

"Sorry, I don't think there's any food in this thing," Alice said, and then she straightened her posture. "And, anyway, I'm not a scullery maid anymore. I'm an adventurer. And once we rescue the Princess, Simon and I will become knights, just like you."

Sir Gawain looked as though he might laugh, but he thought better of it.

"Fair enough," he said. "You have traveled to this far planet, rescued me, and destroyed the tiger. In my eyes, you are worthy."

Simon felt so proud he thought his chest might burst. But he knew he had a long way to go before becoming a knight. He slipped into the pilot's seat. "All right, let's get to the next planet."

"Try coordinates X-15, Y-15," Alice suggested. "Those are next on the list."

"Sounds good," Simon said. He pulled the LAUNCH lever, and the rocket zoomed into space once more. This time, there were no robot beasts guarding the planet. The words APPROACHING THE JUNGLE PLANET appeared on the control panel.

Simon landed on a platform in the middle of the jungle. He, Alice, and Sir Gawain peered out the window.

They were in a jungle, all right—a mechanical one. The big pink flowers growing on the ground below them were made of metal, and the stems were springs. The leaves on the trees were big, green gears, and they powered swinging platforms that stretched across the jungle.

"At least it's not cold out there," Alice remarked. "And I don't see any metal tigers."

"Don't jinx us!" Simon warned. "What if there's something worse?"

"Perhaps I should stay back and guard the ship for you," Sir Gawain offered nervously. "I am still weak, and I would only hinder your efforts."

"What about you, Merlin?" Alice asked. The robot owl shook his head from side to side in response.

"See? Merlin doesn't like the look of this place, either," Simon remarked.

"I'm sure we'll be fine," Alice said. "Let's go find the Princess!"

They left the ship and walked out onto the platform. Another swinging platform came right toward them, and Simon was about to step on it when Alice stopped him.

"Look, down there," she said, pointing. "Do you see something glowing?"

Simon looked down and nodded. "If it's glowing, like the shield, it might be useful. Let's go see."

He jumped from the platform into the center of a giant pink flower, and Alice followed him. Then they grabbed on to vines dangling from the tall trees overhead and shimmied down to the forest floor. They didn't have to go far before they saw the green glow ahead of them.

"It looks like a weapon," Simon said as they got closer. The glow came from a long, pointy stick with a handle. "It's Sir Cador's Laser Lance! One of the Three Mystical Weapons of Arturus!"

Simon grabbed the Laser Lance and held it in his hands. "This is amazing," he said in wonder. "To think, Sir Cador held this!"

"Then where is he?" Alice asked.

They both gazed around the jungle floor. "I don't see any sign of him," Simon said. "Maybe we should start heading up."

They quickly climbed back up the vines, grabbing tree branches when they could for support until they reached a swinging platform.

"This is easy," Simon said, once they were safely aboard. "We just wait for this platform to meet the next platform and step right across."

"Whee!" Alice cried, jumping onto the first platform.

They crossed from platform to platform and ended up on another large, stationary platform in the trees. Waiting to greet them was a knight in green armor.

"Sir Cador!" Simon cried.

"Simon the stable boy? It is good to see you," Sir Cador said, a smile growing on his face. "And Alice from the Castle. Good day, milady."

Alice blushed a little as the knight bowed to her.

"The King sent us to find the Princess," Simon explained. "We found Sir Gawain on the Ice Planet, but we didn't see her there."

"I believe I have finally found her," Sir Cador said. "She is being held in a cage guarded by a fearsome beast. I tried to battle it, but I dropped my lance. And I have been stranded so long that I am too weak to retrieve it."

"We'll battle the beast for you," Alice said. "Simon already defeated a Tiger Copter."

Sir Cador nodded. "Then I wish you both luck. The beast is that way."

He pointed down the platform, and Simon and Alice slowly walked to the edge. Simon handed the lance to Alice.

"I got to use the shield before," he said. "It's only fair."

Alice's eyes widened. "Thank you," she said,

gently swinging the lance in front of her. "I feel like a real knight!"

The platform ended in front of a huge nest with four eggs. They could see the bottom of a cage hanging from a tree branch, but they couldn't see what was inside.

"I don't see any beast," Simon said.

"Then that just makes this easier," Alice pointed out. "Let's get to that cage."

Emboldened by the lance in her hands, she jumped on the first egg, and Simon followed. Suddenly, he felt something nipping at his heels. He looked down to see that a huge mechanical baby bird with a sharp beak had popped out of the egg!

"Hurry! The egg's hatching!" he yelled.

They jumped from egg to egg, and when they reached the last one, they took a final leap and landed on the platform around the cage. But there was no Princess behind its wooden bars.

"It's a winged horse!" Simon cried. He had grown up around horses but had never seen one as beautiful as this. "And it's not a robot, either."

"It's called a Pegasus," Alice said. "And we should save it!"

The wood bars were easy enough to break. The

pair entered the cage and climbed onto the grateful horse's back.

"Fly away!" Simon commanded, and the horse spread its wings and flew out of the cage. At that moment, an earsplitting cry rang through the jungle.

"Look out! The mother Phoenix is coming!" Sir Cador yelled.

Chapter Seventeen

Into the Volcano

"A Phoenix! That's a legendary bird," Alice said.

Simon nervously looked down at the giant eggs. "If it's the mother of those things in the eggs, then I'm guessing it's a really *big* bird. You'd better fire up that Laser Lance."

Alice pointed the Laser Lance forward and switched it on. The weapon glowed bright green.

"It's so beautiful," she said.

"And powerful. When it's green like that it means it's fully charged," Simon explained. Alice might know all about Mordred and strange creatures, but when it came to the knights and their weapons, he was the expert. "I'll steer the Pegasus, and when we see the Phoenix, just aim and shoot."

They could see a flash of orange metal in the distant sky. The Phoenix was getting closer. Above them, the sky grew dark, and ominous black clouds hung overhead. After the storm clouds, a small army of metal, melon-size yellow birds was flying toward them, blocking their path to the Phoenix.

"Better use the lance now!" Simon cried.

Pew! Pew! Pew! It took only a short laser blast from the lance to take down each bird. Once hit, the birds spiraled down to the jungle floor.

Simon was impressed. "You're an expert shot, Alice!"

Alice smiled, pleased. "That's from years of shooting pebbles at the rats in the Castle basement. The place is full of them."

Zap! One of the thunderclouds overhead released a jagged yellow lightning bolt, and Simon steered the Pegasus out of the way just in time.

"That was too close!" Simon cried.

Now they could make out the body of the Phoenix, another mechanical beast.

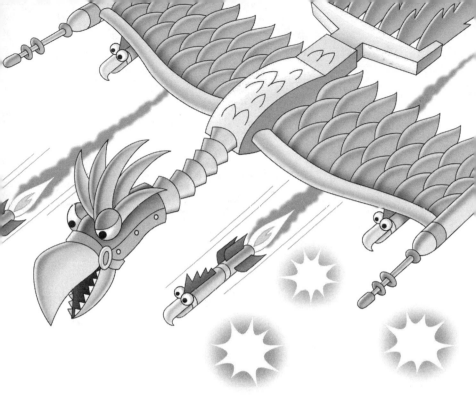

It looked like a fighter plane with a fierce bird's head
and wings made of feathered metal. Attached to each
wing were three long missiles, each one topped with
a bird's head—and the Phoenix was starting to fire
them.

Whoosh! One of the missiles sped toward them,
and Simon pulled back on the reigns to fly above it.
When the next one zoomed at them, Alice blasted it
with the Laser Lance, and it dropped from the sky,
spewing smoke.

"Huzzah!" Simon cheered.

"Uh-oh. The lance isn't green anymore," Alice said.

"It will recharge," Simon told her, remembering the shield. "We'll just have to dodge the missiles until it does. Come on, Pegasus!"

And then the robot Phoenix swooped toward them with a horrible, metallic shriek.

"Shoot!" Simon yelled.

Pew! Alice got off a shot that hit the Phoenix's wing—but didn't do any damage.

"I think it needs to be charged more," Alice called to Simon. "We're going to have to dodge this thing before I can shoot again."

Simon dove down quickly, avoiding another missile launched by the Phoenix. The mechanical beast lunged toward them, and Simon brought the Pegasus high above it. By now the lance was glowing green once again.

"It's fully charged!" Alice yelled.

"Right!" Simon steered the Pegasus so that they were face-to-face with the Phoenix. Alice quickly launched an attack.

Boom! The bird's body shook and gave off an orange glow.

"It's working!" Simon cried.

They kept up the strategy, Simon flying over the Phoenix and then circling back down until the lance was charged again.

Boom! Another hit. The Phoenix began to shake, and some of its metal feathers fell off.

"Huzzah!" Alice cheered. She steered away from the Phoenix, once again circling until the lance glowed green.

Boom! The Phoenix shook violently, flashing with bright orange light. The remaining missiles harmlessly dropped to the ground. Then the robot's head fell off, and the body plummeted to the jungle floor and crashed.

"We did it!" Simon yelled, and they flew back to the platform and landed in front of Sir Cador.

"It was a trick! The Pegasus was a decoy!" the knight said, shaking his head. "That was well done. I will accompany you in your search for the Princess."

When they got back to the rocket, Sir Gawain was surprised to see his comrade enter with Simon and Alice.

"Have you not found the Princess?" Gawain asked Cador.

"No," Cador replied. "Only another trap set by the evil Binary Bard."

Simon interrupted them. "One of the aliens on the Pewter Moon was talking about the Binary Bard. I'm confused. I thought we were looking for Mordred."

"We have found no sign of Mordred," Cador told him. "But a new villain has emerged—the Binary Bard. He is the creator of the hideous mechanical beasts we have found."

"But isn't that the same thing Mordred is famous for?" Alice pointed out. "He made robot beasts, too."

The two knights looked stumped. Sir Gawain shrugged. "Listen, we're just trying to find the Princess. Does it really matter who kidnapped her?"

Alice realized there was no use arguing with the knights. Simon looked at her and shrugged, then slid back into the pilot's seat. He hit the LAUNCH lever and piloted to their next destination: the Fire Planet. Through the window, it was easy to see how the planet got its name. The whole globe pulsated with red and orange flame.

They landed on a small rock sticking out of the bubbling lava that covered the planet's surface. Through the window, they could see the landscape, studded with volcanoes and geysers spewing steaming lava.

"I think we should check out that big volcano just

over there," Simon said, pointing.

"How?" Alice asked. "That bubbling liquid will melt us like cheese fondue."

Simon pointed to the geysers. "See how there is a flat stone on top most of the geysers? We can jump on the first stone, and then when the geyser pushes us up, we can jump to the next and then the next, until we get to the volcano."

Alice nodded. "That should work." She turned to the two knights. "Let me guess. You guys want to stay here and guard the ship, right?"

"We will guard it with our lives!" Sir Gawain and Sir Cador promised.

"Right," Simon said. He took a deep breath. "Okay. Let's go save the Princess!"

"She's got to be here," Alice said hopefully. "It's our last stop."

A blanket of blazing heat hit Simon and Alice as they stepped out of the rocket. Red-hot lava bubbled all around them. The nearest geyser was a short jump away, but the lava raised the stone on top up and down, up and down.

Working together, Simon and Alice crossed the lava by timing their jumps from stone to stone perfectly. The last jump deposited them at the mouth of the big volcano. It wasn't steaming, like the others on the planet.

"It must be dormant," Alice guessed. "That means it won't erupt. At least I hope it won't."

Simon grabbed her hand.

"There's a ledge down there," he said. "Let's jump."

They jumped together and landed on a ledge of dark brown stone.

"It's like a maze in here," Alice remarked, gazing down into the belly of the volcano. Ledges of rock jutted out from the volcano's walls, creating a treacherous, zigzag passage to the bottom. "We might as well go down."

Alice jumped down to the next level. Simon jumped down next to her—and was immediately hit by a hot wave of steam that glittered with yellow flecks.

"Hey!" he cried, ducking. "I thought you said this volcano was dormant."

"I guess there are updrafts coming from the magma way down below," Alice said. "When we see one coming, we'll just avoid it."

Luckily, the yellow flecks in the hot steam made it easy to spot when an updraft was coming. The two friends jumped and ducked, jumped and ducked, until they reached a long, cool passageway at the bottom of the volcano.

"What's that?" Simon asked.

A strange creature was blocking their path. It looked like a snake made of brown rocks linked together. Each rock had one unblinking eye.

"I don't know," Alice admitted. "But at least it doesn't have a mouth or fangs. I think we can jump over it."

Alice took a running leap, and the rock creature formed itself into a circle and blocked her path, knocking her backward. Then the rocks broke apart and quickly began to reassemble.

"Tricky little critter," Alice said, dusting herself off. "Hurry, Simon! Before it puts itself back together."

They both ran as fast as they could and leaped over the creature. They both landed on the other side and kept going—and ran right into a knight wearing orange armor.

"Greetings, strangers," he said. "I am Sir Pelleas. I was sent to find the Princess, but alas, I have failed."

"We know," Simon said. "The king sent us to find you. We found Sir Gawain and Sir Cador. They are safe and waiting in our ship."

Sir Pelleas raised his helmet. "I thought you two

looked familiar! I'm glad you're here. A fearsome beast dwells in the cave, and I believe he holds the Princess captive. The beast is too strong for me, but perhaps the two of you can defeat it. Here, take my arrow."

The knight handed Simon the blue Ice Arrow. Another mystical weapon! Simon studied its blue, shining arrowhead in wonder.

"You should use the weapon this time," Alice said. "I'll back you up."

"Godspeed, warriors!" Sir Pelleas called after them.

Simon and Alice slowly made their way into the dark cave.

"Do you think it's another trick?" Alice asked.

"Probably," Simon said. "But we have to try."

Boom! A fireball came out of the darkness, landing at their feet. The cave lit up, and they saw the creature that had thrown it—a green mechanical dragon with spikes on top of its serpentine body. Instead of legs, the bottom of the beast was made up of the treads of a battle tank.

"Oh no!" Simon wailed. "It's a fire-breathing dragon!"

Chapter Eighteen

The Crystal Gate

Boom! Boom! The dragon, which sat on a high platform, shot two more fireballs at them. Simon and Alice each jumped in a different direction to avoid it.

Simon waited until the dragon stopped shooting fireballs and then hurled the Ice Arrow at it. The arrow struck the dragon but didn't seem to do any damage. Then it magically appeared back in Simon's hands.

"It didn't work!" Simon cried, dodging another fireball.

"Try shooting it into its mouth!" Alice yelled back. "The fireballs are coming from inside the dragon's belly, right? I bet the arrow will cool them down."

Simon waited until another fireball whizzed by and then jumped out from the safety of the cave wall. He hurled the arrow again, but the dragon quickly closed its mouth.

"It's impossible!" Simon wailed. But then he spotted something over by the dragon's tail—a lever.

"Alice, I have an idea. Can you jump over the

dragon and pull that lever?" he called out to his friend.

"No problem!" Alice answered.

She jumped up and grabbed a metal chain hanging from the cave ceiling. Then she swung from chain to chain until she was safely behind the dragon. She ran underneath its tail and pulled the lever.

The dragon's mouth opened, and Simon leaped forward and hurled the arrow into the fiery opening. Steam came from the dragon's nostrils, and a fireball popped out—but this one was weak and fizzling.

"I think it's working!" Simon said as the arrow magically appeared in his hand again. "Again!"

Alice pulled a lever, and Simon aimed another arrow at the dragon's mouth. This time, the beast began to tremble. More steam came out of its nostrils.

"One more time!" Simon yelled.

Bam! With the help of Alice, Simon got one more Ice Arrow down the dragon's throat. The mechanical beast began to rumble and shake.

"Alice, get out of there, quick!" Simon warned.

Alice jumped up and grabbed a chain just as the metal platform holding up the dragon cracked in two. The beast slid into the bubbling lava below. Then she swung across the chains and landed safely next to Simon.

"We did it!" she cheered, and the friends hugged.

They left the cave and approached Sir Pelleas.

"We defeated the beast," Simon reported. "But there's no Princess in there."

"We have been fooled by the Binary Bard!" the knight said. "He must be hiding the Princess elsewhere. We must find her!"

Without waiting for Alice and Simon, he began to swiftly climb out of the volcano. They caught up to him and led him to the rocket, where the knights welcomed Sir Pelleas with hearty slaps on the back. While the three knights talked about their adventures, Simon slid into the pilot's seat and quickly checked the ship's stats.

"Let's go back to the Pewter Moon and recharge our shields," he said. "We need time to figure out a plan, anyway."

He steered back to the Pewter Moon. While Simon worked on the shields, Alice walked over to the knights and politely curtsied.

"Excuse me, noble knights," she said. "We need your help. We looked for the Princess on three different planets, and all we found were three traps set by the Binary Bard. Do you have any idea where he might be?"

"I have heard that he lives in another galaxy," Sir Cador offered.

"Yes," agreed Sir Gawain. "To enter the galaxy, one must have a Key to the gateway."

"Well, I heard that the Key to the gateway is on a large asteroid," Sir Pelleas said.

Alice looked at Simon, who nodded. "Okay. So to find the Binary Bard, we need to get this Key." He hit the LAUNCH lever. "Let's go hunting for an asteroid!"

As they launched into space once more, Alice and the knights gathered around the control screen.

"The screen says we're approaching an asteroid belt," Simon explained. "Everybody hang on!"

The rocket lurched as Simon took a sharp turn to avoid bumping into an asteroid. Through the ship window, they could see a maze of bumpy brown rocks floating in space.

Sir Gawain turned a light shade of green. "I much prefer battling on the good earth of Arturus," he said.

"Don't worry, we'll get home soon," Simon said confidently. "Look!"

In the distance, they could all see a large asteroid with a crystal tower embedded in it.

"That looks like a magical gateway to me," Alice said. "Simon, I think you've found it!"

The ship lurched again, sending Alice and the knights tumbling across the rocket ship.

"Oh, dear!" Sir Gawain moaned, gripping his stomach.

"Huzzah!" Simon cheered, straightening the ship as an asteroid zoomed past. Then she steered straight for the large asteroid and landed safely on the bumpy surface.

"To the gate!" Sir Pelleas cried, rushing to the door, and the others followed behind—including Merlin this time.

They climbed up the jagged side of the Crystal Tower. At the very top, they found a gold Key embedded in a large chunk of crystal. Words were inscribed on the large crystal tower behind the Key:

"When the five knights of the Quest are gathered, the Chosen Ones may pull the Key from the stone."

"Ah, yes, that must be us," Sir Gawain said. He put a hand on the Key, and Sir Cador and Sir Pelleas quickly added theirs.

"For Arturus!" they cried as one, and then they pulled with all their might.

The Key didn't budge.

Sir Gawain frowned. "There must be some mistake. Once more, men!"

The knights pulled at the Key until their faces were red as lava, but they could not move it.

Alice cleared her throat. "I mean no insult, good knights, but I think the Chosen Ones must be me and Simon," she said politely. "After all, we're the ones who defeated the beasts."

The knights looked at one another uncomfortably.

"How can that be?" Sir Pelleas asked. "You are not knights."

But Sir Cador bowed to them.

"You have proven your bravery many times over," he said. "You are, indeed, the Chosen Ones."

Simon and Alice looked at each other and grabbed the bottom of the Key.

"One . . . two . . . three!" Simon cried, and they pulled up on the Key. It slid effortlessly from the stone.

"Incredible . . ." Sir Pelleas said in disbelief.

The writing disappeared from the crystal tower, and a swirling vortex appeared on the tower's face. Alice grabbed Simon's hand.

"Here we go!" she cried, and they jumped inside with Merlin flying behind them.

The vortex spat them out in what looked like a medieval city with stone towers and buildings. They jumped from a rooftop onto the street, where they found a pretty young woman wearing a purple and yellow gown and a conical hat with a white veil flowing from it.

"Hooray, you've found me!" she cried.

"Princess Elyana!" Simon yelled.

"Yes, and I am being held captive here," she replied. "I need the Three Mystical Weapons to destroy this place so that we can all escape."

"Of course," Simon said. He took the Force Shield from his neck and handed it to her, along with the Ice Arrow. After another curtsy, Alice handed her the Laser Lance.

The Princess began to laugh—and then her voice became deep and evil. Before their eyes, she transformed from a beautiful girl into a man wearing a purple and yellow jester's costume. Half of his face looked like a metal robot face, with one glowing red eye.

"You're not the Princess," Simon said accusingly. "You're the Binary Bard!"

"Ha-ha-ha!" the bard laughed. "I must thank you for bringing me the Three Mystical Weapons!"

Chapter Nineteen

Mecha Mordred

"He tricked us again!" Alice yelled angrily.

"With the power of the weapons I'll create the ultimate energy source," the Binary Bard crowed. "Now nothing can stop me from taking the kingdom— and the universe! Bwaaa-ha-ha!"

Then it looked as though he simply faded away, disappearing behind a stone door with twenty rectangular panels. Alice pounded on the door with her fist.

"Come on, open up!" she yelled.

The panel she hit flipped over, along with several other random panels. The flip side revealed what looked like part of a picture.

"It's a puzzle!" Simon exclaimed. "I bet if we solve it we can get in."

He and Alice took turns pressing on the panels, watching carefully to see which ones flipped each time. Seconds later they had solved it, revealing a picture of the Binary Bard wearing a king's crown.

Underneath were the words, "King Mordred, Master of the Universe."

"I knew it!" Alice cried triumphantly. "The Binary Bard and Mordred are the same person! He's the one who attacked Arturus. And he's the reason the Princess is missing."

"Maybe now we'll find out why she went with him," Simon said.

They easily pushed open the door and found themselves in a large room that looked like a medieval cathedral with ornate stained-glass windows. But the room was filled with strange machines. On a platform in the center of the space was a cylinder filled with green liquid—and the Princess was inside!

"Help!" she screamed. "Mordred captured me and plans to make me his bride so he can rule the universe as king!"

"So you didn't escape with him because you were in love?" Alice asked.

A dark look crossed Elyana's face. "Mordred was not the man I thought he was. And now he must be stopped. Please hurry!"

"We can climb up and save you!" Simon said bravely.

"It might not be that easy," Alice said, pointing.

A giant robot marched into the room. The friends quickly realized it was a robot suit with a human pilot inside. Through the dome on top of the robot's head they could see Mordred working the controls. A green glowing orb floated above the dome, and the mecha robot held a jagged green sword in each metal hand.

"You fools! Nothing can stop the power of my creations!" Mordred cried.

Hoot! Hoot! Merlin flew off Alice's shoulder and soared toward Mordred.

"Merlin! You traitor!" Mordred cried. He moved the robot's arms so that the swords twirled in front of him, protecting the dome.

Merlin kept trying to fly near the green orb, but Mordred swatted it away each time.

Merlin crashed into the robot's body again, and this time, several round bombs tumbled out. The owl swooped down and grabbed one of the bombs and then flew up above the mecha's head and dropped the bomb on the green orb.

Boom! The orb flashed red and then turned green again.

"Huzzah for Merlin!" Alice cheered.

Merlin swooped down again and picked up another bomb.

Boom! He hit the green orb again. Annoyed, Mordred shot a red laser beam from the mecha's forehead. The beam hit the robot owl and sent it spiraling across the room.

Alice looked horrified. "Merlin, no!" she yelled. The owl might be made of metal, but she had grown as fond of it as she would any living pet.

While Alice stared at Merlin, hoping for some sign of life, Simon ran to the platform. The sides were smooth and slick. "There's no way to climb up!" he yelled.

"Climb up the robot to get to me!" the Princess called down.

"How are we going to do that?" Simon asked, looking nervously at the spinning sword blades blocking his way.

Alice tore herself away from the owl and looked at the robot.

"I think it's like a lot of the traps Mordred has set," she said thoughtfully. "Like the lava geysers and the platforms in the jungle. It's all about timing."

Simon nodded. "You're right. We can do this."

They cautiously approached the Mordred Mecha-Bot. The two swords were spinning in circles. Simon watched carefully, and when the swords were pointing to the ceiling, he hopped in front of the robot. Then he jumped up onto the robot's body, below the dome, and then hopped up to the dome. His last jump landed him on the platform with the Princess. Alice landed right behind him.

"We've got to get her out of this thing," she said, searching the cylinder for a way to free the Princess. There was a glowing green button on the base, but when she pressed it, nothing happened.

"I can try to figure this out," Alice said. "But we still have to escape Mordred."

Simon gazed around the room, taking in their options. His eyes narrowed when she saw a chandelier hanging from the ceiling.

"I think I know a way to distract him," Simon said. "Watch this!"

Simon jumped to the chandelier and swung from it, just like he had swung from the rafters of the mill so many times back in Arturus.

"Mordred, I am Simon of the Stables!" he called out. "And I am here to defeat you!"

Mordred turned and stomped toward Simon. The red laser port on the dome began to glow. Then a laser beam shot out, aimed right at Simon!

"Simon, watch out!" Alice yelled.

Chapter Twenty

Two Knights to Remember

Simon moved to the right as the laser beam struck the chain holding up the chandelier. He safely jumped to the floor as the chandelier came crashing down—right on top of the Mordred Mecha-Bot!

The glowing green globe tumbled from the top of Mordred's dome. With no more power, the robot began to shake and steam.

On top of the platform, the green light in the base of the cylinder holding the Princess went dead. The green liquid drained, and Alice was easily able to open up the cylinder, setting the Princess free.

Mordred jumped out of the ruined mecha and raced toward the big green orb.

"The orb is mine!" he yelled.

"I don't think so!" shouted Princess Elyana.

With an angry look on her face, she jumped down from the platform, crashing right on top of Mordred. Then she flipped him over her shoulder, leaving him dazed on the floor.

Stunned, Simon and Alice ran up to her.

"Mordred deceived us all," the Princess said. "He would have succeeded in his plans if it weren't for you two. Thank you for finding me."

Simon was staring at the Princess. He had never been this close to her before. She was so pretty—and so tough at the same time.

Alice nudged him. "You should see what she looks like when she eats a jelly doughnut," she whispered. "What a mess!"

Princess Elyana touched the orb. "This orb will restore power to Arturus. Without it, Mordred will be trapped here forever."

"Then let's get back to Arturus," said Simon. He gave a slight bow. "Our rocket ship awaits you, my lady."

"Just one second," Alice said. "I'm not leaving without Merlin."

Hoot! Hoot! The robot bird flew up and landed on Alice's shoulder. Merlin looked battered but okay.

"*Now* we can leave," Alice said.

They returned to the rocket with Princess Elyana and the orb. She tearfully greeted the three knights. Simon motioned for Alice to take the pilot's seat.

"Your turn," he said.

Alice grinned and took the controls, easily finding the coordinates for home on the control screen. The rocket was a lot more crowded than when they had started, but it wasn't a long trip. As they zoomed through space, Simon and Alice told the Princess the story of their amazing journey.

Alice steered the rocket to a smooth landing right in front of the Castle. As the passengers climbed out, curious villagers began to gather, chatting with excitement.

"The knights have returned!" someone shouted. "And the Princess is with them!"

A huge cheer went up from the crowd as the Castle guards ran to fetch the King and Queen. They soon came running down the stairs, breathless. The Queen let out a cry when she saw her daughter.

"Elyana! You are safe!"

The King and Queen hugged the Princess, sobbing.

"Three cheers for the knights!" someone yelled. "Huzzah! Huzzah! Huzzah!"

Sir Gawain, Sir Cador, and Sir Pelleas climbed to the top of the Castle stairs and waved, grinning. Simon and Alice began to get caught up in the fast-growing crowd, getting pushed and shoved.

"I guess they forgot about us," Simon said glumly.

"It's not fair!" Alice fumed. "I am *not* going back to that kitchen!"

Suddenly a green glow fell over the crowd, and the villagers hushed. Princess Elyana broke away from her parents and held up the orb.

"Not only have I and the knights returned safely, but power will be restored to Arturus!" she announced. "And while our knights traveled far and were indeed brave, they are not our only heroes today. Let us cheer for my rescuers, Simon of the Stables and Alice of the Kitchen!"

There was a confused murmur in the crowd, but Princess Elyana persisted. She motioned for Simon and Alice to stand by her.

The friends pushed their way through the crowd and stood next to the Princess.

"These two brave hearts traveled into the fabric of the sky, battled monsters, and defeated Mordred to save me!" she said. "They are worthy knights of Arturus, if my father shall grant them that honor."

"Indeed I will," the King said. "In fact, I promised that I would. Simon and Alice, kneel before me."

Trembling, the two friends knelt before the King. He touched each one on the head with his royal scepter.

"I hereby knight you, Sir Simon and Sir Alice of Arturus," he said.

"I will protect the kingdom with my life," Simon promised.

"As will I," Alice said.

"Then stand and let your kingdom greet you!" the King said happily.

Sir Alice and Sir Simon stood and faced the crowd that was now cheering for them as loudly as they had cheered for the other knights.

"Is this really happening?" Alice asked.

"It is," Simon said. Then he grabbed her hand. "Come on, let's go to the stables."

"I thought you never wanted to go back there?" Alice wondered.

"Not to shovel manure," Simon said. "But for another reason."

"What's that?" Alice asked.

Simon grinned. "Now that we're knights, we get to have horses of our own!"

"Huzzah!" Alice cheered, and the two friends ran off, ready for their next adventure.

Turn the page for a sneak preview of

available now!

Chapter One

Pirates

"Ahoy there, mateys," Owen Christopher said as he peered through a spyglass toward the port town of Fort Ridley. In the distance, he could barely make out the buildings of his hometown through the thick black clouds that filled the sky.

It had been months since he had signed on as cabin boy of the zeppelin *Aurora*, and Owen was feeling a bit homesick. Since they were scheduled to pass by his home of Fort Ridley, he had put in for shore leave—more accurately, land leave, as the *Aurora* spent all its time soaring through the skies.

"Are you sure you want this time off?" Captain Arthur McCrea asked. "Fort Ridley looks to be a bit"—McCrea hunted for the right words—"down at the boot heels."

Owen leaned over the side of the bow as the airship approached the edge of the black clouds. "That's smoke," he said. "I thought there was a storm brewing."

"Smells like gunpowder to me," McCrea added. "Someone's been firing off cannons."

"I can't see anyone down there," Owen said. "And it doesn't look like there are any ships in port. I wonder what happened to the navy."

Captain McCrea pointed further out into the harbor. "There's one ship down there. And she's flying the Jolly Roger."

"Pirates?" Owen asked. "There haven't been pirates in Fort Ridley since before I was born. Quick, let's get to the port. I have to find out what's going on."

"I can't take the *Aurora* through that smoke cloud," McCrea said. "We're not getting anywhere near that port."

"But, sir," Owen pleaded. "That's my home. I have to get down there."

McCrea puffed out his chest and placed his hands on the ship's iron railing. After a moment, he shook his head and let out a small sigh.

"Okay," the captain relented. "I can make a quick pass over the pier, but we can't stick around. Once you're out, you're out."

"I understand," Owen replied. He was anxious to get down to Fort Ridley.

"There's just one more thing," McCrea added. "And you're probably not going to like it . . ."

McCrea was *right*, Owen thought as he shimmied down the long stretch of rope and into the black smoke cloud. *I don't like this one bit.* He could hear the wind whipping past him as the *Aurora* made its descent into the skies above Fort Ridley. The zeppelin would only be able to stay in the cloud for a few moments, so Owen had to be ready to let go of the end of the rope and jump off as soon as they were over the piers.

Owen held his breath to avoid inhaling the soot from the cloud as he lowered himself one hand after another. He couldn't make out the docks or even the end of the rope.

"All right, son," McCrea called out from above. "It's now or never."

Below him, Owen saw only darkness mixed with the occasional swirl of grayish light. He tried to focus on something. Anything. For a brief moment, he thought he saw the wooden planks of the pier below his feet. Knowing this was his only chance, he let go of the rope.